MEANWHILE
THERE WERE DRAGONS

A NOVEL

A TRAVELING SHOES PRESS BOOK

MEANWHILE
THERE WERE DRAGONS

A NOVEL

JON CHRISTOPHER
ILLUSTRATIONS BY ZARA KAND

TRAVELING SHOES PRESS
PO BOX 332
Pioneertown CA 92268

Meanwhile There Were Dragons
ISBN# 978-1-732-92050-7

First Edition | 2018
Edited by Jean-Paul L. Garnier
Illustrations by Zara Kand
Book design by Jon Christopher

Dedicated to my Uncle Jim,
who introduced me to hockey.

CONTENTS

-1-
TINY DRAGONS

No one noticed the dragons when they first appeared – no one but Jonas Knight. They were so small, about the size of a house fly. Jonas noticed them the first time they landed on the windowsill of his cabin. Jonas was a hermit and lived tucked away remotely in the San Bernardino Mountains.

The dragons were so small that Jonas had to get out his big magnifying glass to clearly see the features on these new visitors that had just shown up at his window on this fine spring morning. *Sure enough*, thought Jonas, *those are dragons.*

Jonas had lived in the mountains for many years and was intimately knowledgeable about all the various critters and insects who were his neighbors. These dragons were like nothing he had seen before. He put out a bowl of bread soaked in kerosene and six tiny dragons came to the bowl and started eating.

By fall a handful of small dragons were regularly feeding at Jonas' cabin. The dragons had grown to the size of large lizards and flew in a group that followed Jonas around as he did his daily chores.

The young dragons playfully shot bursts of flames into the air as they flew around. Jonas had put out more than a few of fires started by the dragons. The dragons were pretty intelligent and seemed to understand when Jonas scolded them about starting random fires. Soon the young dragons started putting their fire breathing skills to use, toasting small vermin and clouds of mosquitoes.

Throughout their first winter the dragons kept on eating and growing. Jonas continued to feed them bread, and anything else he was eating, soaked in kerosene. The dragons loved the kerosene and would belch little puffs of smoke after eating.

The dragons were starting to develop individual features as they grew, so Jonas gave them names. Abraham was the first one to start growing a beard and was the darkest of all the dragons. Luther was the first to grow prominent horns on his head, he had two. There were three female dragons who had all retained the translucent wings from when they were small. These three were Celeste, Deirdre, and Edie. The smallest dragon of the group was a male named Nathan, he had stripes of red and yellow that ran the length of his body. Nathan liked to ride on Jonas' shoulder and was Jonas' constant companion and guardian.

By spring the six dragons had grown to the size of large dogs and each one had the wingspan of an eagle in flight. They all had a distinctly reptilian look and if a person saw one flying they would not have mistaken it for a bird. Soon the dragons formed into mating groups and flew off into the mountains, first Luther and Deirdre, followed by Abraham with Celeste and Edie. Only Nathan stayed behind with Jonas.

There could be much speculation about where the dragons came from, but in my opinion, they came out of the aether, out of the mists of possibility, out of the quantum background noise that forms the scaffolding of all reality. Dragons are such a strong

thought form, such a universal component of our collective consciousness, that they were birthed into our collective reality was
only a matter of time. What I mean by this is, it had to happen
sooner or later. One moment dragons did not actually exist except
in the imagination, then the next moment they popped into reality.

Unbeknownst to Jonas, numerous tiny dragons had suddenly
come into existence all over the planet, thousands of them, many
of them didn't make it past the tiny stage. But out in the remote
areas, far from the reaches of humankind and their insecticides,
small families of dragons were beginning to form. It would be a
while before the arrival of the dragons would be noticed by the
people of the planet. A few things needed to happen before the
world would be ready for that.

-2-
CELESTIAL KNIGHT

Jonas' older sister, Celestial Knight, or Celeste for short, lived in the nearest town, fifteen miles away by four-wheel drive jeep. She drove out and visited him every month or so and brought necessary items, like cooking supplies. In exchange she would pick-up several pounds of some of the best mountain-grown marijuana available anywhere. It had a high that was euphoric like a mountain vista, with a creative spark that was long lasting, and when it wore off you landed softly, ready for another flight.

Celeste had a dedicated group of customers for Jonas' mountain-grown herb. Every time she brought back a few pounds of the JK Special, as she called it, her friends would get together for a happy hour and pick up their supply.

Jonas was a legendary figure among the town's people. He had been living out in the woods for over twenty years. He had only come into town three times during those years. Once to help his sister move, once he suddenly appeared one afternoon looking for a bottle of whiskey, and once he was seen just walking down the small highway that ran through town. That's it.

Each time he'd been seen in town he spoke to at least one person but none of those people will repeat what he said. Sherry Oscar, who works at the drug store, saw Jonas when he was walking along the highway on his way to get a bottle of whiskey and ran over to see if he was okay. They were seen talking for over five minutes. At first Sherry denied even speaking with Jonas. Later she said their conversation was too private to share. It was like Jonas had been reading her mail.

Celeste had driven out to visit Jonas many times while the dragons were growing up. She kept her mouth quiet about what she saw. Jonas named the biggest female dragon after his sister. She had visited a few days after Jonas had first noticed them and had seen them feeding at the kerosene and bread bowl.

"Those are bugs, Jonas," she said.

"No, they are dragons, for sure. Look at the way they love kerosene. Only baby dragons do that." Jonas replied.

"Where did you get that crazy information?"

"What? I thought everyone knew that..."

Months later, when the dragons had grown to the size of large lizards she had to acknowledge that they might, indeed, be dragons. They did have wings and breathed little clouds of fire while they flew in a little thunder that followed Jonas around.

Just a side note – a *thunder* is the proper name for a group of dragons. As you can imagine, we'll use that term often in the story ahead.

And like I said, Celeste kept quiet about what she saw while visiting Jonas. Who would believe her anyway?

It was in the spring of the following year, when the dragons left to go mate in the mountains, that Jonas told Celeste about Malthusius.

-3-
MALTHUSIUS

Jonas and Celeste sat on his deck overlooking the valley below while sharing a joint of JK Special. It was a clear and bright morning. Jonas' mind was occupied with thoughts about a creature named Malthusius.

"Have I ever told you about Malthusius?" Jonas asked his sister.

"Who?" replied Celeste.

"Malthusius," repeated Jonas, "an intelligence that exists on this planet that is far beyond the mind of humankind," Jonas began, as he got ready to unfurl a small speech about Malthusius.

"This intelligence lives beneath the waves of the Pacific Ocean in a kingdom of its own. He, and I'll use 'he' for convenience, was brought into existence by a primordial race of creatures long before humans roamed the galaxies." Jonas paused to take a hit from the joint and handed it to his sister.

"Humans roamed the galaxy? I don't think that's happened yet," interjected Celeste taking the joint from Jonas.

"We, Earthlings, haven't roamed the galaxy, per se, but other humanoids have..." Jonas trailed off, giving his sister a look that said, "please hold your horses while I continue my story."

"Primordial entities conceived of a massive creature, a cephalopod of huge proportions," started Jonas once again.

"What's a cephalopod?" asked Celeste, who knew nothing about the oceans, or its various creatures.

"A cephalopod is like an octopus, or a squid," answered Jonas, getting a little annoyed at constantly being sidetracked from the story he was trying to tell. Celeste passed the joint back to Jonas and he took another hit.

After a moment a nice relaxed vibe settled over the deck. Jonas began to unroll his tale once again.

"As I was saying, once there were a number of primordial entities who roamed the earth, sky and waters. No one knows where they came from because they had existed as long as the earth itself. These entities conceived of creatures wherever they roamed and life sprouted up around the earth, everywhere. New species popped into existence. The truth of the matter was that these primordial entities had extremely powerful mental capabilities and could control quantum reality.

"There came a point when the primordial entities began to realize that their era, their time, was coming to an end, and they put their minds together to conceive the greatest beast of all time. The result of their conception was Malthusius, a being with vast mental powers over life on the planet. I'm talking about a seriously powerful creature. Malthusius was a mind frequency manipulating master. He could alter space and time if he really gave it a try, know what I mean?"

Jonas paused to take one last hit off the joint, he offered it back to Celeste but she'd had enough. She sat back, her arms crossed, a skeptical look on her face. Jonas noticed her skepticism but continued.

"Malthusius was a benevolent overseer of the planet for millions of years. If you could call him benevolent. Some people might have a different opinion," Jonas looked at Celeste and shrugged his shoulders and continued, "From deep under the waves of the ocean he controlled most of the evolution of life on the planet. He manipulated life and he destroyed life. When he left the ocean and came onto the land, thousands of octopuses and other cephalopods like the Kraken came with him, devouring every living thing in their wake. I'm telling you, cephalopods are dangerous – don't trust them.

"After humankind arrived at this planet-"

"What do you mean, after we *arrived*?" interrupted Celeste, "I thought we evolved here."

"Hell yeah we came from another planet, didn't you know that?" Jonas gave his sister another sideways glance, "It was after the war between Malthusius and the dragons, which everyone now calls dinosaurs. The dragons almost killed Malthusius, but eventually he hunted every one of them down until the ancient race of dragons were extinct."

"Dragons? Like your little friends?"

"Yup, dragons, like Nathan here, and they are smarter than you could ever imagine," Jonas pointed at Nathan who seemed to be sleeping peacefully on the railing of the deck.

Nathan lifted his head for a moment and looked at Celeste. A small trickle of smoke rose from his nostrils and Celeste knew the dragon had been listening to their whole conversation.

"This creature, Malthusius, has been alive for a billion years," continued Jonas, "but he sleeps for really long periods of time. Malthusius has been asleep for the last fifteen thousand years, at least that's what the records show."

"What records?" Celeste was feeling more than a little skeptical about her brother's story, in spite of the dragons.

"The Akashic Records, of course."

"The what?"

"The Akashic Records, you know, the record of all knowledge,

of all time, recorded in the aether, the Akashic field. Where do you get your information?" Jonas shot Celeste a look she couldn't figure out. She figured she'd just look up the Akashic Record online later, when she had some time.

"The records also say that dragons will appear when it's time for Malthusius to awaken," continued Jonas.

"Like now?" asked Celeste, growing a little more interested.

"Yes, like now."

The two of them continued to talk about Malthusius into the night. The conversation drifted to the nature of cephalopods, the Kraken, mysteries of the deep and what the Akashic Records showed was possible in the near future. Celeste spent the night in Jonas' spare bedroom, and dreamed of deep underwater worlds full of monsters, strange and weird.

After a nice breakfast Celeste drove back to town, a bit unsettled after talking with her brother. Jonas watched her go, happily thinking about his plans for the near future.

Jonas washed up the morning's dishes, straightened up his small cabin, left a note on the bed that said "Gone trout fishing in America", locked the door and headed down the front path. Nathan flew over his head and Jonas stuck out his arm for Nathan to land on. Once the dragon had settled on his arm, Jonas vanished, dragon and all.

-4-
IN THE ZONE

Jean-Paul was in the zone. There were just a couple minutes left in the hockey game and the other team had pulled their goaltender to add an extra attacker on the ice. The score was one to nothing and both teams were facing off half a sheet of ice away from JP.

The other team had fired thirty-six shots at JP so far and he had stopped every one. JP watched the puck in the hand of the linesman who was about to drop it. JP saw it all happen in slow-motion, the drop of the puck, the flash of sticks, the ice flying from skate blades, the quick one-two pass up the ice and then the slap shot from just inside the blue line. JP's glove hand shot out and grabbed the puck out of mid-air, dished it off to the side of the net for his defenseman who started the play going the other way. That was shot number thirty-seven, not that JP was keeping track. The number didn't matter at the moment. The only number that mattered was on the clock ticking down to zero on the giant screens over center ice.

JP's eyesight was extremely good, and when he was in the zone he saw things much faster than the average human. JP lived

for being in the zone. It was a place of serenity and grace, everything was so effortless.

After a quick, forced turnover, the other team brought the puck back to the offensive side of the ice and began their attack. Taking advantage of their extra attacker they passed the puck around the perimeter to tire out the defensemen with a short game of keep-away. Suddenly a shot came from down low and deflected off a stick in front of the net. JP was already a step ahead of the play and got his right skate stretched out to block the shot. The puck bounced to the corner and another shot came from down low. JP reached up from where he was laying on the ice and caught the puck and held on to it for a faceoff.

JP faced five more shots before the game ended. Five shots and five stops. His teammates mobbed him when the final buzzer sounded. It was the team's sixth victory in a row and JP's third shutout in the last four games. Nearly 17,000 fans were on their feet clapping and chanting JP's name.

It was near the end of the regular season and the playoffs were just around the corner. After tonight's victory the Anaheim Ducks secured their position in first place in the Pacific Division of the National Hockey League. In fact, they had more points than any other team in the NHL, which meant home ice advantage for the entire playoffs. Last year the Ducks had gone as far as the finals of the Stanley Cup, only to be defeated by the Montreal Canadians. This year was going to be different. JP could feel it. And he would know, he's the one who was in the zone.

Several hours later, Jean-Paul Lafleur had talked to the press, showered, changed into his street clothes and was on his way home. Home was a sparsely furnished four bedroom house he rented in Yorba Linda. JP had moved there a couple of months ago after he had been called up from the Duck's farm team.

The last two years had been a pinball of trades that landed JP in the starting position as goaltender for the Anaheim Ducks. He had been an All-Star goaltender when he was in Juniors, but that seemed like a lifetime ago, so much had happened.

He had been signed by the Boston Bruins straight out of Juniors, and played for a year in their minor league team, the Providence Bruins. It was a horrible year. His mother died of liver cancer while he was two thousand miles away playing hockey. He had been really close with his mother and talked with her nearly every day. Not on the day she passed away, he had been playing a road game and didn't get to say his final good-bye. Her death was like a large stone thrown in JP's small pond of life, the ripples continued for months. JP's older brother Remy took some time off from teaching college to fly out and live with JP during the year in Providence.

JP was traded to the St. Louis Blues late in the season and promptly dealt to the Vancouver Canucks to be a backup goaltender during the Stanley Cup playoffs. During the fourth game in the second series of the playoffs, the starting goalie gave up three quick goals and was pulled by the coach. It was JP's moment to shine. JP quickly stopped an onslaught of shots on the goal and helped settle the game down. The Canucks battled back and won, the score was 4-3 at the end of regulation. The team the Canucks were playing was the Anaheim Ducks, and they had been shopping around for a new goaltender.

After the playoffs were over the Ducks traded several players for Jean-Paul and sent him to their farm team, the San Diego Gulls, where he was starting goaltender. The season had been good to JP, and the Gulls had gone on several winning streaks and were leading the league in goals-against average. JP had four shutouts with the San Diego Gulls before he was called up to the big club in January, as starting goaltender. That's when he had moved into this house in Yorba Linda.

He had rented furniture for the living room, dining room and only one bedroom. The rest of the house was rarely explored, and unfurnished. Once JP got home he grabbed a beer, a Lagunitas IPA, from the fridge and settled down on the sofa. He had recorded the game on his TV and proceeded to have several beers while he watched the night's game being replayed. His mind was still in the zone, all he thought about was the game.

-5-
MS. TURNER

"Turner," called a voice from behind one of the windows. "Turner," the voice called louder. Paige looked up from her phone where she had been checking her social media news feed.

Paige was in the Social Security office in Yucca Valley and the voice was trying to get her attention. Paige gathered her purse, phone and paperwork and went to the window where the voice was attempting to make its way through a small, grated hole in the glass. The voice belonged to a plump lady name Marge who sat on the other side of the window.

Marge disliked her job at Social Security and the people who sat down in front of her window. Twenty years of working at a variety of Social Security offices from Maine to the Mojave had worn her out. She was only hanging in there for retirement and the benefits.

"We just need you to fill out a bit more paperwork," Marge said, "and we need you to see our physician for an evaluation."

Paige had spent months trying to get disability and was tired of filling out paperwork. The process had been nothing but paperwork and more paperwork.

"I have my own doctor." Paige told Marge, "He's filled out all the paperwork you guys gave me last time."

"Do you have those forms with you now?"

"Yes, right here." Paige held up a folder containing the paperwork.

"Slide them through," said Marge.

Paige slide the forms through the metal tray under the window.

Marge looked over the forms and told Paige she'd be back in a moment.

Paige waited over ten minutes for Marge to come back to the window. Marge had gone to the bathroom, while she was there she had touched up her makeup. She had stopped by the lunchroom on the way back to the window to eat a cookie she had been eyeing all morning. She lingered for a few minutes in the lunch room to check her social media news feed on her phone. One of her co-workers had passed through the lunch room, and they talked about horses for several minutes. Her co-worker could talk about horses until the cows come home. Finally Marge wandered back to the window, still holding the forms in her hand. She had her "serious look" on.

"You still need to see our physician. Their office will mail you an appointment. Don't miss that appointment or your claim will be automatically denied."

Paige sighed, thanked Marge, gathered all the paperwork and left.

Paige's home was parked in the parking lot. It was a 2002 Chevrolet Express van conversion with over 120,000 miles. Paige called her Bessie. Bessie had taken Paige all over the country and back to the hi-desert, more than once.

Paige's copilot was a St. Bernard and Mastiff mix, a giant of a dog named Rufus. Rufus was four years old and weighed more than Paige. Rufus slept on the bed in the back of Bessie and kept an eye on Paige while they traveled.

Bessie had been parked on Paige's friend's land in Joshua Tree for the last six months. Paige's friend was Remy Lafleur, Jean-Paul's brother. Remy was an ethnobotanist who specialized in psychedelic plants and the tribes that used them.

Remy was secretly in love with Paige and had been for years, but he also believed in free love and having no strings attached. Remy let Paige park on his land whenever she wanted and helped her out as much as Paige would let him. Paige was pretty independent and tried to make her way in the world on her own. She *almost* made a living making dream catchers and selling them at festivals and gift shops as she traveled around the country.

Paige liked Remy, but not romantically. He was more of a brother to her, they had known each other since high school. Remy and his brother JP, who was twelve years younger than Remy, had immigrated to Southern California from Canada during Remy's sophomore year of high school. He and Paige had a number of classes together and over the semester they had become good friends, even though Paige was dating one of the stars of the basketball team. Back then Remy had long hair, listened to Pink Floyd and hung out with the smokers. He liked to take acid. He was intensely interested in psychedelics.

After high school and after the basketball player was out Paige's life, Remy got her stoned for the first time. They almost kissed that night but neither of them made the first move, instead they talked for hours about life and what the future might hold. That was in 2003. That was before Paige was diagnosed with bi-polar disorder. That was before a whole series of bad decisions.

-6-
DER

Eugene, Oregon was missing one of its most flamboyant char-
acters. Derringer Brautigan, or as his close friends called him,
Der. Der was in Long Beach, California, preparing for the gay
pride festival, which was coming up in a month.

Der had beautiful hair. He loved his hair and had let it grow
down to the middle of his back. He wore it in a macho style, like
some romance novel cover come to life. Der was the third cousin
of the late, famous novelist Richard Brautigan, and looked a lot
like him.

Der hated his name – Derringer. His father, who had been a
sheriff in Oregon, named him after the famous pistol, *the Derringer*. Der was a pacifist and hated all guns. His father was shot and
killed on the job when Der was six years old, and that had deeply
effected him. He was raised by his mother and her lesbian lover.
They raised Der to think outside the sexual box, and he did.

Der's current boyfriend was a black cross-dresser named Paul
LePaul. Paul lived in Long Beach and Der visited whenever pos-
sible, which was at least once a month for the last half a year.
Chartreuse was Paul's favorite color, and he had dyed his hair that

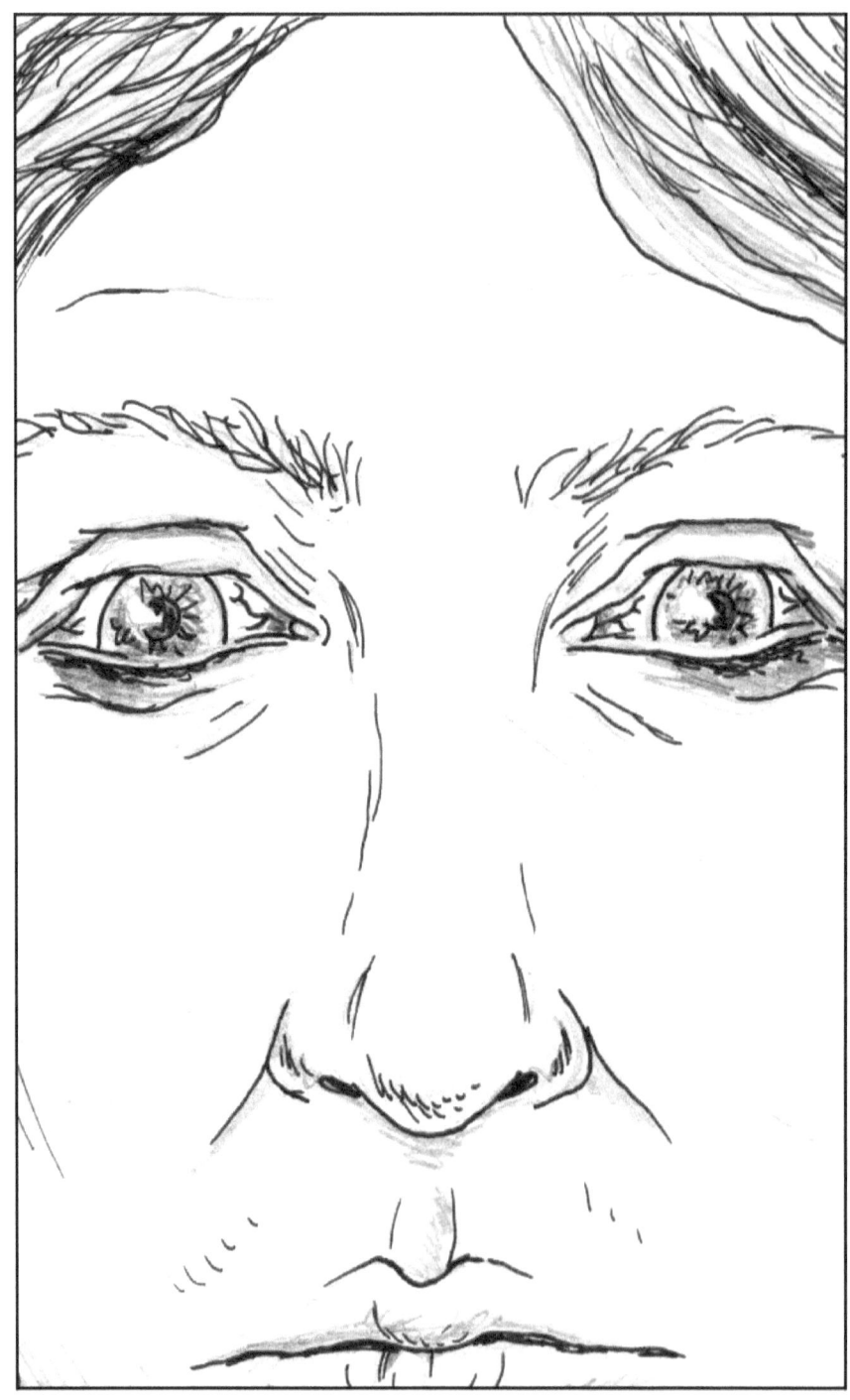

color. He loved Der's hair and wished he could dye Der's hair chartreuse too. Of course, it wouldn't look as good on Der as it did on Paul.

Paul lived on Broadway and the noise of the traffic woke Der first. It was the Monday after a long weekend of partying. Paul's bed was in the middle of the living room of the one bedroom apartment and Der laid awake for a while, listening to the sounds of people, cars and buses passing by. His home in Eugene was in a quiet residential area and he never heard the city sounds like he did when he stayed at Paul's apartment. As he listened to the traffic he let his mind wander and it wandered off into a field of worry and stayed there for a while.

He worried a lot about a number of things, like about the mole on his inner thigh. It was weird and changing shape. He imagined that it hurt, but it didn't really. He was sure it was cancer. He was worried about how to pay rent next month. He worried that his latest client was going to hate the look he had come up with for the website he was designing. He was worried about his teeth. He was worried about the pain in his left foot, in his big toe. He was worried that it might be gout. His head hurt and he had a bad hangover.

After a while Paul stirred and mumbled something about breakfast. He got up and Der watched him as he walked across the room on his way to the bathroom. Der stopped worrying for a moment and reflected on the past weekend. It had been a blur of parties and pills – speed and Xanax – and lots of alcohol. Most of their behavior had been over-the-top and irresponsible. Now, in the light of a sober, hung-over, Monday morning the memories of the weekend seemed cheap and plastic, all confetti, gaudy makeup and loud outfits.

When Paul came back to bed Der got up and went to the bathroom. He looked in the mirror and wondered about the face he saw looking back at him. The face was not the fresh eighteen year old he imagined himself to be. The face was in its early-forties, boyish and an old man at the same time. His eyes had the smudged remains of eyeliner he had worn the night before. The eyeliner made his eyes dark and hollow looking. This was the first time Der had looked in the mirror and said to himself, "I'm getting old."

Getting old meant a lot to Der. It was a big line in the sand he was trying his best to avoid. *Old was the land of unwanted people. Old is not young, and to be young is everything. Old is the end of the line, over the hill and out to pasture,* Der thought while he washed his face and did the best he could to remove the eyeliner.

Der spent a while combing his hair, slowly. For some reason he never worried while he combed his hair. It was a moment of peace.

When Der emerged from the bathroom Paul was already busy making breakfast, and the coffee was ready.

"Honey, you want bacon with your eggs?" Paul asked Der when he walked into the kitchen to get his coffee.

"Yes. Crispy please." replied Der.

"Eggs over easy?"

"As always."

"It'll be ready in a few, hun."

Der wandered into the living room with his coffee and found his phone. He checked his social media news feed while he waited. His favorite hockey team, the Anaheim Ducks, had won the night before. Their new goaltender, Jean-Paul Lafleur, was playing fantastically. Der watched a video of the highlights of the game.

"Breakfast is ready, hun," Paul called from the kitchen.

"You want to go to a hockey game?" Der asked Paul, walking back to the kitchen.

"Oh honey, I'll go anywhere with you."

"Have you ever been to one?"

"No, but there's always a first time."

"Hockey is so cool live. You have to watch it in person to really understand how exciting it is."

"Sign me up, honey, lets go."

Der went online to order tickets for a game the next week. It was the last home game of the season, before the start of the play-offs. Der was surprised the game wasn't sold-out. The best seats he could get were way up in the "nose bleed" section.

"Do you have binoculars?" he asked Paul when he finished ordering tickets.

"Yes, why?"

"We're gonna need them to see the ice."

-7-
THE SONG OF MALTHUSIUS

Deep below the waves of the Pacific Ocean a great and terrible presence was waking up, much like Jonas had predicted to Celeste. Malthusius' mind shook off the many millennia of slumber and started to think and feel again. His mind reached out to take in the current state of his world. Malthusius sensed the presence of billions of humans on the surface of the planet. He felt the presence of millions of species of animals. He felt the ocean creatures, and the sky creatures. He felt the presence of dragons. He felt the presence of creatures we cannot perceive. He felt into the fifth and sixth dimensions.

His eight legs, each over seventy-five feet long, started to move and taste the ocean around him. He was inside his giant castle of corral and stone. His seaweed covered castle was several hundred feet tall and rested in a deep, underwater canyon. As Malthusius awoke he sent a mental call out to the Kraken. The Kraken were the loyal slaves and followers of Malthusius. Or, at least they used to be.

It had been fifteen thousand years since Malthusius had last called the Kraken and things had changed. The Kraken were giant octopus-like creatures, usually over fifty feet long and were the well known sea monsters of legend. They loved to swim up from under a ship, wrap their tentacles around their victims and drag the ship and its crew down to the depths below, where the Kraken would make a quick meal of the drowning crew members. The Kraken, who were rather intelligent, had nothing but contempt for the human race.

Over the last fifteen thousand years the Kraken had grown to think of themselves as their own masters. There were about a hundred members of the Kraken society and they lived off the coast of Norway and Greenland. They ate fish, sharks, whales and occasionally humans when they got the chance to pull a ship down.

Malthusius knew exactly what was going on with the Kraken. He had slept and woken many times over the last billion years. Every time the Kraken had wandered off and become independent and every time he had needed to call them back and put them under his control, again. There were very few, if any, creatures that could resist the direct call of Malthusius.

The probing call of Malthusius unsettled the whole Kraken society. The call was persistent and subtle, it got under the skin of the Kraken in a pleasant and persuasive fashion. The Kraken found the call irresistible and soon they were on their way to the castle of Malthusius, deep under the Pacific Ocean.

It took several weeks before the Kraken arrived at the castle of Malthusius. By this time the call had softened their minds to any resistance to Malthusius' will. Malthusius had spent the time waiting for the Kraken to show up by continuing to learn about what was going on in his world. He considered the whole planet as his world and you could say he read the mind of the world.

It is well-known that we humans, as a species, have a collective consciousness to which we all contribute. Creatures like Malthusius can read the vibrations, the sounds, the thoughts of the collective consciousness like we read the morning newspaper. He could read the general themes, the memes of humanity, he could feel the mood of the planet. He could feel the wars, the strife, and the violence. He could feel the weight of the age, the pollution and abuse of the planet. A lot of stuff had happened to his planet while he was asleep. Malthusius was not amused by what he found.

So Malthusius started to sing. His song cut right through the collective consciousness and began to resonate with the planet. He sung a mournful song. He sung a deep and low song. The frequency of the song centered around 7.83 Hz. The pitch rose and fell in Fibonacci sequences. There were movements of passion and terror, brief moments of rapture mixed with long movements of disgust. The world of humans did not know it yet, but their new master had awakened and was beginning to sing songs that would hypnotize the whole world.

Hugo Branson was one of the first to fall under the spell of Malthusius. Hugo lived in Montana and ran an internet podcast out of his spare bedroom. His podcast was called *My Country, Right or Wrong*, a pseudo-patriotic broadcast from the extreme right. To say that Hugo was a white nationalist was to understate his mindset.

Hugo always began his podcast with his personal slogan: "We're white, we're right, and we're on the air tonight." Hugo thought his slogan was pretty damn clever.

It was shortly after Malthusius began singing that Hugo fell under the spell of the song. The song somehow hit a deep chord within him and Malthusius' message to the world took shape inside his mind – now he couldn't stop thinking about trash in the ocean. For several days he thought about little more than ocean trash and in his mind formed a clever and simple way to clean the oceans.

Hugo's next podcast thoroughly confused his core audience of nearly a thousand listeners. Hugo preached for almost an hour about the evils of ocean pollution and explained his plan to clean up all the waste and plastic.

One of Hugo's listeners was surprised, pleasantly surprised, by what he heard on Hugo's podcast. This listener was Bob Candler, a member of a media watchdog group called ALERT. ALERT wasn't an abbreviation for anything, the group just liked to use all capital letters in their name.

Bob Chandler had been listening to Hugo's pseudo-patriotic and racist podcasts for over a year, documenting the various offensive things Hugo would say. Tonight's podcast had been like no other *My Country, Right or Wrong* podcast Bob had heard.

"We are all humans and we have failed our planet, our home," began Hugo at the start of the podcast, instead of his usual slogan.

"We have nearly wrecked the world and the time has come to fix the problems we have created."

The next hour was filled with valuable information including Hugo's, or should we say, Malthusius' simple plan for humans to clean the oceans.

Bob Chandler listen to the podcast twice before he emailed its link to his supervisor at ALERT, with his observations. The supervisor listened to the podcast and forwarded the link to Bud Henry, the top dog at ALERT. Bud also ran an ocean salvage company. Hugo's plans made perfect sense to Bud. Bud saw dollar signs in his head while listening to Hugo's podcast.

-8-
TEACHER PLANTS

Over the last number of years Remy Lafleur had personally tried ninety-seven different psychedelic compounds, both synthetics and from plants, or plant mixtures. Many he had taken more than once. His consciousness was strong and he loved the challenge of being a pychonaut. His mind had been to places and conversed with intelligences that most people can barely conceive of, let alone imagine. Several times he had been on research missions deep into the Amazon to take psychedelics with different tribes of the forest.

The tribes didn't call their medicine psychedelics or drugs, they invariably referred to them as *maestras*, teacher plants. The teacher plants taught them everything they needed to know. The teacher plants had told the shamen of the tribes that Remy was coming to see them, and to show him what they knew.

Teacher plants are of a level of intelligence that's far beyond the minds of humans. They don't experience time the way we do. All of time is presently existing to most teacher plants, as this is the actual reality of things – it's much different than our nice, orderly perception of the flow of time. Teacher plants bridge our apparently physical world and the actual cosmos around us.

The actual cosmos is considerably stranger than we perceive, not surprising, considering our limited range of perception. For instance, many scientists have speculated that there are eleven dimensions, where as we only perceive four of these areas of space, time and consciousness. This is just one example of the vast distance between what we see, smell, touch, taste and hear, and the actual world as it truly exists outside of our narrow band of awareness.

Remy was familiar with the broader range of reality. As I mentioned, he had conversed with a number of intelligences. I call them intelligences because they weren't creatures or persons as most people would understand them, but disembodied entities that could take whatever shape they chose. Different plants each have their own intelligences that come to guide the person who has ingested them.

Remy used magic mushrooms for recreational purposes and as an instructive teacher plant. He usually had weekly adventures with the mushrooms. After eating about five or six grams of mushrooms he'd spend some time with the green mushroom elf that would show up in the middle of the trip. Remy and the green elf were old friends by this point in his life, having been on many trips together. Remy called the elf "Sam". The elf didn't appear to mind being called Sam. He didn't seem to have a name of his own, or he never offered it to Remy.

Remy was a professor at Cal State University Long Beach and taught botany. As a world-class ethnobotanist he could have taught at Harvard or Yale, but he preferred the low key profile he maintained at CSULB. Not only did he avoid the limelight, but he liked to spend his time out in the hi-desert, and Long Beach was close enough to Joshua Tree to visit whenever he liked. There he had a five acre parcel with a two bedroom house and an extensive cactus garden full of psychedelic plants. Paige Turner had been taking care of his cactus garden for the last six months. It was the most stable six months Paige had known in the last decade, thanks to Remy and his magic mushroom plan.

As an experiment Remy had given Paige a supply of magic mushrooms so she could take a micro-dose every three days. The micro-dose didn't get her high, but over the last few months their experiment seemed to be helping Paige's moods to stabilize. Even the endless paperwork of applying for disability was manageable, which was a world away from where Paige had been the year before.

The previous year had been a disaster. Paige had been living in Connecticut with Phil Berger, a guy who was hooked on Oxycontin. She spent a lot of time drinking cheap red wine, and taking Ativan, which a doctor had prescribed for her anxiety. Because of the Ativan she blacked out often and her memory had big gaps of time missing. She had an accident in Phil's car and didn't remember it happening. While on a manic she took to shoplifting for a while and had been caught. She had to spend 30 days in the county jail. She got out of jail just in time to stop Phil from selling Bessie. Thankfully Phil really liked Rufus, Paige's dog, and took great care of him the whole miserable year.

Paige left Phil shortly after Halloween and headed back to the Mojave. Remy had been truly happy to see Paige again. He was just about to leave for a month, to Ecuador on a research trip for an upcoming book, and needed someone to watch over his cactus garden. Paige had agreed to house-sit while he was gone.

"Have you taken mushrooms lately?" Remy asked Paige one evening before he left for Ecuador.

"It's been years," replied Paige, knowing that Remy was talking about magic mushrooms. "I used to like mushrooms a lot. But I only took them about five times. I think twice was with you."

"I read a study recently that suggested that mushrooms can be helpful to people with depression. It said the mushrooms help create new pathways in the brain, new ways of looking at things," Remy suggested.

"I have bi-polar disorder, not depression," responded Paige.

"But you have depressions, right?"

"It's part of the illness."

"I was just wondering something..." Remy proceeded to explain the ideas he had about using the mushrooms in very small doses as a mood stabilizer and anti-depressant. He had an idea how it could work, and it was unlikely to cause any harm. Magic mushrooms are generally safe to use, especially in such small doses. Paige figured she didn't have anything to lose, and agreed to be Remy's test subject for his theory.

That had been six months ago, and Paige was thinking clearer than she had in years. It was so natural that she rarely thought about it. Every three days, as I mentioned, she took about a half a gram of mushrooms with her breakfast. She never really felt the effects of the mushrooms and just went about her daily activities. Activities that usually centered around watering Remy's cacti and making dream catchers.

Paige used to think there was something mystical and spiritual about dream catchers, but now she was a little more cynical and commercial about them. To her they were road cash.

Dream catchers were originally created by some native tribes to hang over the cradles of children for protection from bad dreams and evil spirits. They are made from a willow hoop, which has a net or web woven inside. Many dream catchers are adorned with feathers and beads. Paige learned to make them from her mother who had been really into native spiritually. Her mom had once been a fortune-teller, tarot card reader and a regular user of the I Ching.

Paige had little interest in spiritually right now. She believed in dogs instead. Rufus was her biggest, most lovable friend, and he was more real than anything. St. Rufus, as she called him, loved Paige in that wonderful way dogs do. Her safety was always foremost in his mind. He and Paige were a pack. And Bessie, she was part of the pack too.

Bessie, if she could talk, would have encouraged Paige to get back out on the road. Bessie was a road machine and that kept her alive. The year in Connecticut had been the longest she had sat in one place. She would tell you she didn't like that situation at all.

-9-
DUCKS VS. OILERS

Der had just enough money left on one of his credit cards to buy Ducks hockey jerseys for him and Paul before the game day. Paul LePaul was going to dress a little more conservative than his usual gowns with sequins, which he had considered wearing at first. His outfit was just a hockey jersey and designer jeans with elaborate silver embroidery down the legs and his big, beautiful chartreuse hair. Der had Lafleur, number 30 sewn on the back of his jersey, Paul's jersey said LePaul, number 69.

The Anaheim Ducks played in an arena that was built in 1993. It used to be called The Pond, but now it is called The Honda Center. The building holds 17,174 people when sold out for a hockey game. The Ducks had been selling out nearly every home game for the last four months. The Honda Center was a great place to watch a hockey game and nearly every seat had a good view of the ice, of course, high up in the building a person might want a pair of binoculars.

The couple arrived at the arena about a half hour before the start of the game. Der parked his rented car in the space he had been directed to by one of the parking attendants with a flashlight.

They got out of the car and joined the throng of people headed into Honda Center. There was a palpable excitement in the air as everyone left their individual lives behind and became a crowd of hockey fans.

Paul was used to the strange looks and stares he drew when he was out in public. Paul loved to let his freak flag fly and didn't mind the stares and rude comments which followed in his wake. "It's the price you pay for being a superstar," was Paul's way of putting it. Der, for his part, just loved the show. "Let those bitches stare," was Der's attitude. It was this combination of superstar and I-don't-give-a-fuck that made Der and Paul LePaul such an outstanding couple.

The two of them bought over-priced beers and hot dogs and made their way toward their seats. The seats were high up near the top of the building. Paul had remembered his binoculars, thank goodness.

"This is a great date idea, hun," said Paul when they had settled in to their seats, "I think I like hockey already and the game hasn't even started."

"Those are the players down there on the ice, they're doing their warm ups," pointed out Der.

"Which team is ours?"

"The one's wearing the same colors we are, silly."

"Of course."

The building had a nice coolness to it and filling the large cavernous space were the sounds of the crowd blending with skate blades against ice, sticks on pucks and a background of rock n' roll music. Der and Paul spent some time just feeling the vibe of the evening while they ate their hot dogs. The arena was only three-quarters filled when the national anthem was sung. Already the excitement level was high. Tonight the Ducks were playing the Edmonton Oilers, so the Canadian national anthem was sung too.

Der and Paul took a selfie and posted it on their social media. Their post said "Go Ducks!!!"

On the ice JP was listening to the end of the Canadian national anthem while standing in the goal crease. His mind quickly locked into the game. Nothing was going to matter for the next three hours but keeping pucks out of the four foot by six foot net behind him.

The first puck that got past JP was a short hopper from near the right faceoff dot that was deflected past his glove hand. The second puck got by JP between his pad and the goal post after being beaten on the play by an obvious fake from the opposing center. The third goal JP actually kicked in the goal himself while trying to stop a rebound attempt. JP could feel that the zone had completely evaporated. The coach pulled him after the third goal came at the 10:42 mark of the first period. Mark Russell replaced him in goal. The Honda Center was almost quiet, the crowd's excitement was nearly extinguished.

"Your guy sucks," whispered Paul into Der's ear.

The Ducks battled hard through the rest of the period and scored a goal just before the end of the first period. During the break between periods Der and Paul went to use the restroom and get more beer.

"Here's to a better second period," cheered Der, bumping Paul's plastic cup with his.

The Oilers came out flat in the second period, and the Ducks kept them pinned up in their own zone for the first five minutes of the period. The frustration wore down the Oilers and one of their defenseman got a hooking penalty. On the ensuing power play the Ducks scored. Fifty-nine seconds later they scored another goal. The game was tied.

By now the crowd was back into the game and the noise level was intense. The sound of the crowd fed the players on the ice and the pace of the game quickened. The flow of the game moved up and down the ice. Paul stayed riveted to the action through the binoculars.

"Oh honey, this game is the bomb," said Paul sometime during the second period.

Just before the end of the period the Oilers scored a goal and the score was 3-4 going into the intermission before the third period.

Time for a quick pee break and more beers.

The Ducks came out like a storm at the start of the third period. They pressed hard for the first ten minutes, but nothing got past the Edmonton goalie. And then the Oilers scored a goal on a breakaway.

The Ducks kept up the attack for the rest of the game, but the game ended 3-5.

The crowd was subdued as everyone slowly filed out of the arena to go back to their cars and their individual lives.

Paul was beside himself. It was the best sports game he had ever seen. Even though the Ducks lost he loved the whole evening. Der was a little glum about the Ducks losing, but Paul's attitude picked up his mood.

"I'm hungry. Let's go to Roscoe's and get some chicken and waffles," suggested Paul as they were sitting in the car waiting to leave the parking lot.

"Sounds delish," replied Der.

-10-
THAT SONG

Cassie Stackwell's given name was Cassidy. She was named after Neal Cassidy, the real-life hero of Jack Kerouac's novel *On The Road*. Despite this little fact, Cassie hated traveling and had only made one semi-voluntary journey in her life, from St. Paul, Minnesota to Joshua Tree in the Mojave desert. That trip was only because her husband, Bob, had insisted upon it. Bob was tired of living in the land of the wind-chill factor and dreamed about the California desert.

In 2014 the Stackwell's sold their house in St. Paul and made the 1,500 mile trek to the hi-desert. They had been married just a few years and the young couple had no children yet. Now they lived on an acre and a half of land close to the entrance of the National Park. Cassie worked as a bartender at the Joshua Tree Saloon.

Cassie Stackwell was well stacked and had long blonde hair. She worked at Hooters in St. Paul before they had moved. She and Bob had met at Hooters. For Bob it had been love at first sight. It took Cassie several months of Bob's persistent attention to go out with him. Their first date was to a Minnesota Wild hockey game.

The Wild had won that night and so had Bob. Cassie and Bob dated for six months before they got married. The wedding was a small affair, with only their families and close friends in attendance.

Remy Lafleur was a regular at the Saloon when he was up in the hi-desert. He had his eye on Cassie Stackwell for quite a while and had hit on her several times. Cassie, who's very familiar with unwanted attention, firmly turned him down every time. Remy, who was a believer in free love, was not the type to be put off by a firm rejection or someone's marital status. In spite of this weird sexual tension, Cassie and Remy had started to become friends over the last year.

Remy had met Bob, her husband, a couple of times and thought he was a real chump. He didn't respect Bob in the least, but they could talk about hockey, which was Bob's favorite sport. Bob was impressed that Remy's younger brother was the starting goaltender for the Anaheim Ducks. Bob, I must point out, is no chump. He was well aware of Remy's interest in Cassie but kept quiet about it, for now. Keep your friends close, and your enemies closer, as they say.

Lately, Cassie had been hearing something that sounded like a song in her head. It had a certain melancholy quality and seemed to continue endlessly. She would hear it when the house got quiet late at night. It was almost like she heard it with her body instead of her ears. The song brought a strange peace to her as she lay in bed listening to it. Several days after she first started hearing the song she asked Bob if he heard it too, but he didn't have any idea what Cassie was talking about.

Cassie hummed the tune she was hearing at random times during the day as she went about her work. One day her co-worker, Brandy, heard her and asked Cassie what song she was humming.

"I don't know," said Cassie, "just something that's been in my head for days."

"It sounds so familiar," replied Brandy, "like I've heard it in a dream."

Brandy looked like she wanted to say something else but Cassie handed her the drinks for the table she was waiting on. Brandy had a reputation for being a little "out there" when it came to talking about dreams, so Cassie didn't pursue the conversation further.

The song continued for a month, not in an annoying fashion, but as a soothing background to life. One day Cassie heard a pop song on the radio that sounded just like the song she had been hearing. It was a new song by Lil' Billy, about cleaning up the oceans, simply called "Ocean". The song was at the top of the charts in spite of its trite lyrics and well-worn beats. The tune seemed to resonate with the public. Cassie convinced herself this is how the song must have gotten in her head. It was something she heard on the radio.

Lil' Billy was amazed at his sudden success. He was a trust fund kid from Newport Beach who could rap and got hooked up with some good musicians that wrote his songs and music for him. Mostly Lil' Billy spent his time collecting tattoos, drinking Jack Daniels No. 7 Whiskey, and buying cowboy hats. Lil' Billy loved cowboy hats. He was cocky and had a rock n' roll swagger. He loved chicks and partying at strip clubs.

Lil' Billy also had a sensitive side, he cared about the ocean. He had asked Mike, the songwriter of the band, to write something about cleaning up the oceans. He kept having dreams about saving the ocean from pollution. He had hummed a little melody that had been in his head to Mike. It was kind of catchy how Lil' Billy hummed it and Mike quickly worked out a little song about saving the oceans that was dripping with sentimentality. They recorded it that night in their band's studio and played the song for their manager the next day. Their manager said the song was going to be a gold hit. He was wrong. The song went platinum.

-11-
CLEAN UP TIME

The ocean was calm and it was a good day to clean up some trash. Bud Henry stood at the side of the boat and looked out at the trash skimmer – the realization of his plans for cleaning up the oceans. Today his team was going to test out the designs based on Hugo Branson's podcast.

Branson was on a boat 50 feet away from Bud ready to begin the test. Hugo was a changed man since his revelation and Bud had hired Hugo to come work for him on his salvage operation as a consultant.

You might wonder what had caused such a change in a lifelong racist. It was the song that Hugo was hearing, the same one that other people were starting to hear, but Hugo felt it very intensely. It was a mournful song about the death of the ocean. It was a song of sadness and hope. It was a song with a plan to save the oceans. Of course, the song itself wasn't causing the changes in Hugo, the song was just the vehicle. In that vehicle rode the hypnotic mental frequencies of Malthusius, who could easily control the minds of humans. Malthusius had plans for Hugo and a few like him. Meanwhile, because of the mind control, Hugo was becoming a much more pleasant human being.

Based on the idea he had gotten from Hugo, Bud had designed a very simple device for skimming the trash off the top of the ocean's surface. This was just the first phase of the plan. His full plan involved cleaning the ocean to a depth of 100 feet, hauling off waste and recycling the vast collection of trash across the Pacific Ocean. Bud figured no one else had the gumption to go out and do the job, so he would do it.

Bud's daughter, Melissa, ran the front office for Bud's marine salvage business – Float'em Enterprises. She had worked in the office since she was in high school and that was twenty years ago. She had seen her dad get involved in some crazy schemes before and she though this one was sure to bankrupt the company. That was before Lil' Billy's song "Ocean" started to climb the charts. Now Melissa was thinking about running an internet funding campaign for the ocean cleanup project.

Melissa got Bud's approval and launched the campaign that weekend. It got a huge boost when Lil' Billy contributed ten thousand dollars and posted on social media about it to his fans. The campaign raised over two hundred thousand dollars within a few weeks. Bud was interviewed on NPR about the project. *National Geographic* got on board and wanted to make a documentary. Soon, a global effort began to emerge to clean up the oceanic messes of the human race.

Now, on this calm day on the ocean, there was an excitement amongst the assembled team of salvage engineers, which included Bud's two sons, Mike and Don. They had gathered off of Catalina Island and were about to dump a ton of plastic bottles into the ocean. The plan was to pick up all of plastic bottles over the next few hours, without scooping up any fish. The goal was to be as minimally invasive to the sea life as possible. *National Geographic* was on hand with a team of marine biologists, various technicians, and a film crew to observe to test.

Mike was in charge of the bottle release team. The bottles had been towed out to sea using a giant net and the idea was to release the net and the bottles would float free and scatter across the water, ready to be scooped up with Bud's trash skimmer. The trash skimmer was nearly 50 feet across and was moved through the water by two cruisers, one at either side of the device. The skimmer consisted of a number of filters, nets, belts, gears and rollers to sort out the trash from the marine wildlife. Even though the device sounds complicated it worked simply and efficiently.

Mike released the bottles and the test began. The current quickly caught the bottles and started to scatter them across the water, as planned. The team waited ten minutes so the bottles could spread out and create a larger target area. After the brief wait the two boats hauling the skimmer went to work. Bud had worked out a cleaning pattern for the boats to follow which would simplify the process. The boats followed Bud's pattern and within a short period of time all the visible bottles, along with a variety of other trash had been picked up by the skimmer. Only a few fish were found when the team went through the collected trash. The skimmer had picked up a ton and a half of bottles and assorted trash.

The test was considered a success, and Bub pointed out later to the *National Geographic* crew that this test not only proved the idea could work, but underscored the amount of trash floating free in the ocean.

Don Henry, Bud's youngest son, was not thrilled by the day's events. He hated being out on the water, he hated his dad's business and he hated the idea of being a sea-faring garbage man. He really wanted to be a lawyer. His mind worked endlessly on ways to sabotage the enterprise.

Hugo Branson was overjoyed at how the day had turned out. Malthusius, who was tuned in to Hugo's brainwaves, had watched the whole event through Hugo's eyes and was also very pleased. His first song had worked great, and he prepared to sing a new song.

-12-
DRAGONS HAVING DRAGONS

Jonas' dragons bred that season, high in the Sierra Mountains. The second generation of dragons were born from eggs rather than merely popping into existence as the first generation had. These dragons were much bigger in size and returned to the water like many of their distant ancestors had done. Dragons are by nature aquatic creatures. Though they are known as creatures who fly through the air and walk on land, they really love to live in rivers, lakes and oceans.

Abraham was now over eight feet long and had a wingspan of nearly twenty feet. Celeste and Edie, his lady dragons, were over six feet long and had laid a dozen eggs each. The eggs were large and the newborn dragons were already two feet in length when they hatched. They were a hungry bunch of dragons and were ready to hunt as soon as they hatched. Within ten minutes of the near simultaneous hatching of all the dragon eggs, a thunder of dragons took to the sky heading for Lake Tahoe.

Numerous people saw the dragons as they approached Lake Tahoe. The thunder dove towards the lake, hit the water and began a feeding frenzy on the brown and rainbow trout. A small number of residents captured bad photos on their phones of the dragons as they flew overhead.

Luther and Deirdre had a dozen offspring of their own and the whole family flew to the Pacific Ocean and took up residence under the waves. Elsewhere, around the globe, families of dragons were breeding, having offspring, and heading toward large bodies of water. The next generation of dragons were even larger than their parents and most were born underwater.

Even though a bunch of photos had been posted on the social media outlets, the reports of dragon sightings were still considered strange and unlikely by most of the world's population. Again, the world would have to wait a bit before they were ready for the dragons.

-13-
THE PLAYOFFS BEGIN

Lil' Billy sang the national anthem at the first home game of the playoffs. JP was starting in goal and was thrilled about hearing Lil' Billy sing. He was a big fan of Lil' Billy's debut album, *Dreamsongs*. JP was pumped up for the game. He knew he wasn't in the zone but he was ready to play some fast and furious hockey.

The Anaheim Ducks were facing the San Jose Sharks, who had barely made it to the playoffs. The Sharks had a number of key players injured and were not expected to get far in the playoffs, but of course, anything can happen once a series gets underway.

After the national anthem was finished JP shuffled back and forth with his skates on the ice in front of the net. He wanted to rough up the ice and create a little snow inside his office in the goal crease. His mind locked into the game.

The Sharks came out strong in the first period and JP was tested quickly and more than a few times before the Ducks seemed to find their skating legs. The Ducks took a penalty early in the first period and the Sharks scored right away. The goal seem to wake the Ducks up and they began to play their game. They quickly scored two goals in five minutes. The score was 2-1 at the end of the first period.

The Duck's coach was not happy when he addressed the team between periods. Nearly every player had made mistakes on the ice during the period and the coach wasn't about to let any mistakes slide – not at this point in the playoffs. This was the beginning of two months of hard fought games while they marched towards the Stanley Cup, *if* the Ducks made it that far.

The coach pointed to a pad of paper nailed to the wall of the locker room. There was a big sixteen on the first sheet of paper. It would take sixteen wins to claim the Stanley Cup.

"I want to tear that page off the wall after the game. I won't settle for less." the coach's voice was stern, his mood unquestionable.

The coach had already led four teams to win the Stanley Cup and he had been hired by the Ducks to do one thing, bring home the Cup.

The Ducks came out like a storm in the second period. So did the Sharks. The pace was fast and furious for seven minutes until the Ducks scored another goal on a breakaway. The goal seem to take the wind out of the Sharks' sails. The Ducks piled on one more goal before the end of the period.

The third period was tightly contested. San Jose took too many chances on the ice and the Ducks scored again, and that's the way the game ended, 5-1.

After all the various Ducks' players assembled in the locker room, the coach walked over to the pad of paper on the wall and tore off the number sixteen. Underneath, in large numerals, was the number fifteen.

"Thank you," was all the coach said to the team and he turned and left the room.

-14-
THE NEW SONG

Rufus was asleep inside Bessie, lying on the bed in the back. The side doors were open, Rufus came and went as he chose. Rufus was having dreams, his paws were moving against the air and he was speaking about something.

"Aww roof grr roof ROOF," Rufus was saying. In his dream Rufus and Paige were holding off a pack of coyotes and Rufus was telling the coyotes that they better back down, now.

It was late-April and wildflowers were everywhere in the hi-desert. Paige was still at Remy's house and there was still no word from Social Security concerning her disability claim. She was reading the news online on the laptop she had bought several years earlier. Her attention was drawn to a story about dragons sighted in Russia. There were several photos taken from a cell phone that were not particularly good quality. In one photo you could see that the dragon, or whatever it was, had a huge wingspan, unlike any known bird.

Paige loved dragons, or at least the idea of dragons. She followed a link at the bottom of the article to a website dedicated to dragon sightings. Some of the photos on the site were amazing –

and if the creatures in the photos weren't dragons, than what were they? They weren't birds.

Rufus had gotten up from his dreamy nap and had come over to where Paige was sitting in a chair on the porch. He leaned his large body against Paige's legs. Paige scratched him behind the ears, Rufus leaned his head back and gave Paige's hand a big lick. Rufus loved Paige as much as a dog could, and that's a lot.

Paige set aside her laptop and picked up a joint from the ashtray. It had gone out after she had taken a couple of hits forty-five minutes ago. She re-lit the joint, took a few more hits and settled back in her chair. The breeze was cool but not too cold. The recent rains had turned the desert green. Rufus chased the lizards that would occasionally run across the porch.

Paige listened to the silence, but what she heard wasn't silence, it was a song, one that had started a few days ago. The song was faint, far away sounding. Paige wondered if she was hearing someone's radio, maybe one of the neighbor's, but the nearest neighbor was a quarter mile away. The song was really pleasant and Paige wished she could hear it a bit louder. It put her in a re-laxed mood. Or maybe it was the joint. Maybe it was both. She closed her eyes and sat listening, trying to hear the song better. The song made Paige think of the ocean, about how beautiful the un-derwater world was. The song made Paige think of peacefully floating on the water without a care in the world.

Paige was not the only person hearing this new song. Cassie Stackwell could hear it, as could one out of every twenty people. Around the globe nearly 350 million people were hearing this song in their heads. The song had a pleasant effect on society. The over-all anxiety level went down and for some reason traffic was mov-ing better on the freeways than it had in years.

Rufus could also hear the song. He didn't know where it came from, nor did he question it, but he liked it, as well as a dog can like music.

Remy was one of the people who could hear this new song in his head. He was at his home in Long Beach where he lived when he wasn't out in the desert. He was awake in bed and listening to the song mingled with the city sounds coming through his bedroom window. The song greatly unsettled Remy. There was something sinister underneath a sugar coating of… Remy didn't know what to call it and turned over in bed. He wished the song would stop but it was endless.

After a while of tossing and turning Remy got up and went to his study to roll a joint. The joint helped Remy to relax but it didn't make the song go away, it made Remy focus on it more. The tune was simple but kept repeating, looping through various scales. The effect was both comforting and intriguing. The mind seemed to want to tune into the song, like a junkie looking to stay high. But something was bothering Remy at the gut level about the music. It was too sweet and comforting for Remy to trust.

Chip Johnson also heard the song. Chip was a psychopath who wore a friendly smile like a mask to hide his contempt for the world. The song was getting under Chip's skin and causing some kind of change. For the first time since he was a child he cried. He cried while reading a story in the newspaper about a homeless man who had frozen to death the previous winter. The story went in depth about the man and how he had died just blocks away from where his daughter lived, unbeknownst to her. She hadn't seen her father in over twenty-five years.

Chip read the story and started to feel tears in his eyes. Confused, he began crying in heart wrenching sobs and snuffles. He felt horrible about the lonely death of the homeless man. He was feeling empathy for the first time, ever.

What Chip didn't remember was an event over a year earlier when he had come out of a liquor store. A homeless man had asked Chip if he had any spare change. Chip had shoved the man to the ground and yelled at him. This is what he had yelled at the home-less man lying on the sidewalk:

"You're a loser and I hope you die."

Like I said, Chip didn't remember this moment and didn't realize it was the same man he was reading about in the newspaper.

The song caused big changes in Chip. Slowly some kind of humanity slipped into his soul and pushed out the psychopathic tendencies. Chip didn't realize this, all he had noticed was that he could breathe better lately, and think better too. Chip ended up quitting his job as a manager at a local bank. He joined the Peace Corp, and disappeared into the Brazilian Amazon. Chip Johnson was just one of many people whose lives were changed by the new song. Around the world many strange, and rather positive changes happened, thanks to the new song of Malthusius.

-15-
AN ILL-FATED ADVENTURE

Newsome Whitmore was preparing his yacht for what turned out to be an ill-fated attempt to sail around the world. Newsome's yacht was the infamous *Sea Queen*. The *Sea Queen* had been the scene of a brutal massacre at sea several years earlier. If you don't remember the news stories, here's a brief recap of the events that unfolded on the evening of July 4th, 2013:

The well-known and popular CEO of Hashtag Inc., J. Allan DuPont, and his forty-seven guests were enjoying a delightful sunset cruise off the coast of California when an unidentified boat pulled along side and five gunmen boarded the two-hundred foot yacht. The gunmen had killed nearly everyone on board. Only Kristen Smith, a call girl, had survived because she had been buried under several dead bodies. Kristen had seen all five of the gunmen. None of them had worn masks or tried to disguise themselves and none of the gunmen were ever found, nor could the police discover a motive. No one on the yacht had been robbed. The case went unsolved.

Nowadays, there were approximately forty-seven ghosts wandering the *Sea Queen*, all in various states of departure from this

plane of existence. The boat had acquired some bad mojo, as they say. Newsome Whitmore was oblivious to the ghosts sharing his yacht. If he had known, he would have thought it made the journey that much more interesting.

Newsome had hired a crew of a dozen weathered seaman to help him on his journey around the world. Newsome was, of course, captain of the *Sea Queen*. His first officer was a Norwegian named Gustaf Johansen. Gustaf had seen a number of amazing things throughout his years at sea, including fantastic sea monsters like the Kraken. The rest of the crew were a mix of hardened criminals and ex-merchant marines.

It was in the spring that the *Sea Queen* headed out of port in San Francisco on its way to Hawaii. The trip to Hawaii was uneventful. The crew settled into the comfortable rhythm of life at sea.

After a couple of enjoyable weeks cruising the Hawaiian Islands, the yacht headed west. The plan was to spend nearly a month crossing the Pacific. That was before the earthquake, the monster and the storm.

The earthquake happened on May 7th and wasn't noticed by the crew of the *Sea Queen* even though it set off a tsunami headed to the Hawaiian Islands. The 8.1 earthquake was located deep undersea near the middle of the Pacific. Geologist were puzzled by the strange location of the earthquake. It wasn't located near any known fault line. The *Sea Queen* was sailing straight towards the epicenter of the quake.

The crew were the first and only ship to ever come upon the newly raised, unnamed island in the middle of the Pacific. An abrupt piece of land had pushed itself up from the depths and consisted of something that looked like a massive, seaweed covered castle several hundred feet tall. The *Sea Queen* pulled into the natural harbor on the south side of the island.

Newsome and a few members of his crew used a dingy to head towards the island to explore the strange castle-like shape. The shape was unusual. The angles were oddly placed and seemed to go the wrong directions. The crew carefully climbed the slippery giant steps that led to the castle. Soon they were confronted by a huge set of doors made of stone. The doors were inscribed with strange and unknown hieroglyphs.

As the crew approached the doors they began to open, swinging inward. Unbeknownst to the crew the flagstones under their feet were pressure sensitive and had started a mechanism that opened the giant portal. Out of the opening came an incredibly horrible smell. Something was moving deep in the darkness beyond the doors. Without warning, giant tentacles came toward the crew as they stood in a state of shock. Three of the crew members were grabbed by the tentacles coming out of the entrance to the castle and dragged inside. The rest of the crew ran like hell back to the dingy. Another member of the crew was grabbed by the giant beast pouring out of the doors. Only Newsome and Gustaf were able to make it safely back to the yacht in the harbor.

Somehow the yacht was able to escape from the island before the strange and terrible beast, Malthusius, came after them. That was just before a huge storm came up. For three days the *Sea Queen* was battered by the fierce typhoon. By an amazing stroke of luck the *Sea Queen* survived and was blown into port in the Philippines. This was the end of Newsome's attempted around-the-world adventure.

There was another earthquake after the *Sea Queen* was in port. Out in the Pacific, the newly raised island, the home of Malthusius, sank back beneath the waves.

-16-
DRAGONS WERE A THING

Paige was quite taken with the story of Newsome Whitmore. She read about him in *Rolling Stone* magazine. Major geologists had said that Newsome's story was impossible. Islands don't raise and sink like he had suggested, but Newsome was sticking by his story.

Paige read everything she could about Newsome Whitmore. This is what it said on *Wikipedia* about Newsome Whitmore:

Newsome Whitmore (1964-) was born the third child of Ellen and Charles Whitmore. Newsome graduated with honors from Harvard University in 1986. Newsome is a world traveler and renowned explorer. He is the discoverer of the Great Pacific Garbage Patch in the Pacific Ocean off the coast of California.

The entry went on to talk about his various expeditions and about his siblings and their various successes in the field of chemistry.

The brief *Wikipedia* entry didn't really tell the story of Newsome Whitmore. It didn't mention that the Whitmore family helped finance the Revolutionary War back in 1770s. Or that Newsome was related to eighteen different U.S. Presidents. And the *Wikipe-*

dia entry said nothing about Newsome's latest girlfriend, Stacy Barnett.

Meanwhile, there were dragons.

The dragons were truly intelligent and avoided humans at all costs. In remote places, caves in mountains, waterholes, ancients forests, lakes, rivers, and deep in the ocean, all around the world dragons had found homes and were growing larger. Twenty and thirty foot dragons were starting to become common.

Paige thought she saw a dragon one afternoon while hanging out on the porch of Remy's house. Something huge had flown across the sky and she wasn't sure what it was. It was, of course, a dragon that Paige had seen. A family of green dragons had moved to a remote part of hi-desert, in spite of the desert's lack of large waterholes. They preferred to stay out of sight, living in an old mine. Occasionally their hunting flights would take them over Joshua Tree.

Far to the north, an amazingly large golden dragon had been born and was growing to an astounding size of seventy-five feet long, from his snout to the tip of his tail. This dragon's name was Alexander, the great and terrible lizard. Alexander had incarnated into our world for one reason and within a short while his purpose would be evident. In the meantime Alexander was concentrated on eating, growing and fighting. Alexander would fight anyone and anything. He enjoyed tormenting packs of arctic wolves merely to provoke a battle. Over time Alexander had become a master of strategy and fighting tactics.

Alexander lived in a huge cave in Mount St. Elias in Alaska. The cave was littered with gold nuggets and that's why Alexander had picked this particular cave. Dragons have an affinity for the yellow metal, and Alexander's cave had a massive vein of gold running through it. He liked to melt the metal with his breath and decorate his scales with thin layers of the melted gold. Alexander shown like some mythical monster as he would fly through the air with his hundred and fifty foot wingspan, sunlight glinting off of him. Alexander was well-revered by the rest of the dragon population and was considered their natural leader. Alexander had a thunder of dragons that would go out hunting with him in the Pacific Ocean. He would lead the group and it was considered quite an honor to be allowed to fly with Alexander's thunder.

Emily Lafleur, a distance cousin of JP and Remy Lafleur, caught some amazing footage of the thunder of dragons flying across the water from the cruise ship, *The Arctic Princess Anne*. Emily was on an Alaskan cruise and it was the fourth day of the seven day adventure. Emily was a documentary film-maker, and had brought her video equipment with her. She had been filming the calving walls of the glaciers when the thunder of dragons came into view, flying straight towards the ship from the direction she was filming.

Over a dozen dragons were clearly in view as they flew over the ship, with the giant, golden Alexander leading the thunder. The sound of the dragon's wings as they flew overhead was like the sound of God pounding on a steel roof. The wind from the dragons passing caused the ship to rock in the water and many people were thrown off their feet. Several people were thrown overboard and one person died from a heart attack.

Emily's footage of the dragons was in high definition and flawless. Over two thousand passengers on the *The Arctic Princess Anne* saw the dragons fly over the ship, but no one had footage like Emily's. Emily posted a small clip of the dragons on her social media page and within an hour her agent's phone was ringing with offers to purchase the complete clip. CNN, ABC, MSNBC, and FOX were all in a bidding war for Emily's footage. Emily's agent handled the bidding war while Emily kept watch on deck in case the dragons returned. CNN won the bidding war, and that night the footage of the dragons went viral. Suddenly, dragons were a thing, a big thing.

Newsome Whitmore announced the following day that he was mounting an expedition to Alaska to locate and capture a dragon. Paige read about Newsome's announcement with great interest. She watched an interview with Emily Lafleur, also with great interest. In her mind, wheels were starting to turn and she thought about a road trip to Alaska. It seemed to her that it would be an easy thing to find Newsome Whitmore and join his expedition.

-17-

EXPEDITION: DRAGON HUNT

A ll the players in the locker rooms were talking about the dragons. Everyone in the Joshua Tree Saloon had been talking about the dragons. *Dragons* was the most searched word on *Google*. This was a new kind of phenomena, and no one really knew what to make of Emily's dragon video.

A number of passengers on the *The Arctic Princess Anne* had posted their own videos of the dragon sighting, confirming what Emily had filmed. Scientists were at a loss to explain what everyone was seeing. Experts had opinions, but they always do. The President of the United States issued a statement neither confirming, nor denying, the existence of dragons, and said they had specialists looking into the situation.

Alexander was unaware of the worldwide stir he had caused when his thunder of dragons had inadvertently flown over the *The Arctic Princess Anne*. If he had known, it would have disturbed him. As I mentioned earlier, the dragons had an instinctual knowledge to avoid humans, because humans are, generally speaking, not very smart, and they can be violent, dangerous and unpredictable. It's not that the dragons disliked humans, they just wished to keep their distance.

Newsome Whitmore did not wish to avoid the dragons. He wanted to find one right away. Newsome had his company, KnewSomeMore Ltd. try to hire Emily Lafleur for his upcoming expedition to hunt for a dragon. KnewSomeMore Ltd. was based in Colorado Springs, Colorado, and existed to make Newsome's expeditions possible.

Emily, who was a bit overwhelmed by the sudden attention she was receiving in the press, accepted Newsome's offer, looking forward to getting away to Alaska again. Emily was hoping she would get some footage that would allow her to make the new documentary film she had in mind, *Thunder of the Dragons*. In the meantime she was reading all she could about dragons, about lizards and dinosaurs.

The team for *Expedition: Dragon Hunt* gathered in a large conference room in Colorado Springs on a beautiful morning. All the members of the team were wearing snazzy new dark blue *Expedition: Dragon Hunt* polo shirts with the expedition logo embroidered on them.

Those present were:

Newsome Whitmore, leader of the expedition;

Barbara Clarence, a fantasy novel writer and self-proclaimed expert on dragons;

George Marks, adventurer extraordinaire and nature writer;

Mike Kleason, professional diver and marine biologist;

Stacy Barnett, Newsome's latest girlfriend, small plane pilot and movie stunt person;

Matt Paulson, navigation and artillery expert;

Dave Kingsley, professional large game hunter and reality TV star;

and Emily Lafleur, whom you've already met.

"Thank you all for coming and agreeing to be a part of this historic expedition," Newsome looked around the room. "We are going in search of dragons, my friends. This is not a journey in search of the fabled Loch Ness Monster or Big Foot. We have actual footage of these great beasts taken by our own team member Emily Lafleur," Newsome gestured towards Emily who was filming the proceedings and continued, "I'm sure all of you have seen this amazing video of the dragons taken by Ms. Lafleur in Alaska several weeks ago."

Newsome gestured again, this time to the large video screen behind him. The complete two minute and thirty-seven second video started to play. First you saw a close up of glaciers calving and collapsing into the ocean, then something dark flew over the glaciers and moved out across the water. The shapes appeared to be a dozen large birds that kept growing in size. The sound of the thunder could be heard in the distance, growing louder. The black birds were obviously not birds and you could start to see colors of red, yellow, green, purple and blue glinting off of the flying creatures.

In the lead was a beast nearly twice the size of the other creatures and colored gold. The creatures flew closer and closer, low across the water with a wake of ocean spray raised by the wind of their passing. The wingspan of the golden dragon was nearly as wide as a Boeing 707. As the dragons drew nearer Emily had been able to get close up shots of individual dragons powerfully flapping their wings as they skimmed across the water. The creatures were unmistakably dragons.

A male voice saying "sure enough, those are dragons," could be heard on the video.

As the dragons got closer they pulled up a bit and just barely cleared the top of the ship as they stormed overhead. In an instant they had passed and the ship was rocking in the water. Off camera you could hear sounds of confusion, wonder and panic. Several people were yelling "man overboard."

The team sat and watched the video several times before Newsome Whitmore continued, "Our plan is to head to Alaska as soon as possible and set up a base of operations in Juneau. My company has already acquired offices for us there. We will start at the Hubbard Glacier where Emily filmed her outstanding dragon footage. We have reason to suspect that the dragons may have flown from the direction of Mount St. Elias. Stacy Barnett, whom some of you have met, will fly us around Mount St. Elias. David Kingsley, how many know David?"

Everyone raised their hands and nodded at David Kingsley.

"Please, call me Dave," said Kingsley, trying to look as humble as possible. Emily zoomed in for a close up of Dave's chiseled face. Something about his smile betrayed his attempt at humility.

"Thank you, Dave," said Newsome.

The meeting continued for forty-five more minutes. Newsome introduced each member of the team and folders of materials were handed out along with *Expedition: Dragon Hunt* sweatshirts and arctic jackets.

-18-
HITTING THE ROAD

The website for KnewSomeMore Ltd. had changed its look overnight. Lately Paige Turner had been checking the site every day and this morning everything was new. The first page had a big banner that said:

EXPEDITION: DRAGON HUNT

Underneath the words was the logo of the expedition; the head of a dragon with its mouth open and forked tongue sticking out. The dragon was black and had red eyes and a red tongue. The head of the dragon was inside of a circle that looked like a compass. Newsome Whitmore paid thousands of dollars to an international graphic design firm to create the logo.

Paige explored the whole website. She was making plans. She made note of the address for KnewSomeMore Ltd. in Colorado Springs. She packed up Bessie and called Remy.

"Remy, I've got to leave for a while."

"Where you going, doll?" Remy liked to call women "doll", "baby" and "honey" because he, mistakenly, thought they liked it.

"Just out of town, highway cruising..." Paige was being intentionally vague, "I have some business in Colorado I had forgotten about and, well..."

"Okay. Is there anything you need for the road trip?" Remy was generous as usual. "When are you leaving?"

"I'm leaving in the morning, and I'm fine. I could use a little gas money."

"Take what you need from the cup in the cupboard. How are the mushrooms working out?"

"The mushrooms are totally helping, I think. Can I take a couple hundred for gas, I'll pay you when I get back?"

"Sure, and come back whenever you want."

The conversation continued for several more minutes. Paige got the money from the cupboard, grabbed a cold beer from the fridge and went to sit on the back patio and watch her last hi-desert sunset for a while. Rufus joined her sitting on the steps of the porch and Paige ran her hand through Rufus' fur.

"Ready to hit the road again, buddy?" she asked her big dog. Rufus seemed to smile at the idea. "How about we go look for Newsome Whitmore?"

Inside Paige's mind surges of dopamine and serotonin had been dumping into her bloodstream and her brain was racing with thoughts. After breakfast the next morning Bessie hit the road, which, of course, made Bessie a happy camper.

-19-
PLAYOFFS, ROUND TWO

JP, along with the rest of the team, was energized after coming off a long seven game series against the Sharks. The Sharks had turned out to be a tougher team to eliminate than was expected. Now JP was warming up for the first game of the second series of the playoff. He was having trouble concentrating and it had to do with the song that kept playing in his head.

Emily's video of the dragons was still big news and the dragons were on JP's mind. He was listening to the song and thinking about getting a goalie mask with a dragon on it – a big orange and black dragon to match the Ducks' colors. The warm up shots kept getting past JP and the coach noticed.

The coach called JP over to the bench and Mark Russell took his place in goal.

"How you feeling?" asked the coach.

"Having trouble concentrating, but I feel good."

"You'll be ready for the start of the game?"

"Yeah, I'll be ready."

JP skated around the ice and back to the goal. He slapped Mark Russell on the goal pads with his stick and resumed his place in his

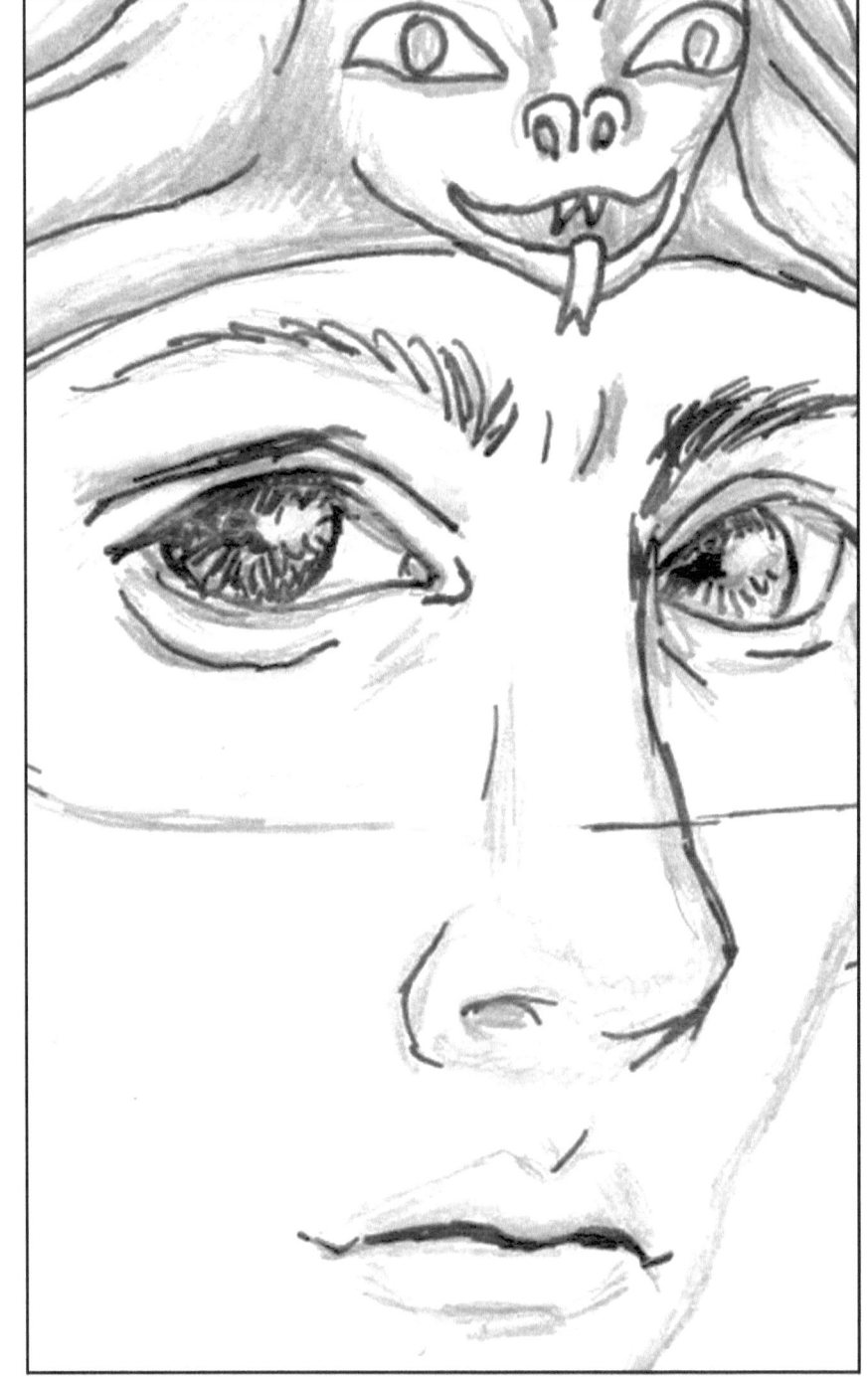

office, the rectangle of blue in front of the net. He settled in and started blocking pucks.

Lang Nichols was the star centerman for the Ducks, he had already scored five goals and had three assists in the playoffs. He was growing a playoff beard and it was getting bushy. Lang skated in on JP, faked one way, skated the other and placed a perfect shot at the five-hole. JP stopped the shot, and Lang skated up to his goaltender.

"Nice stop. How you feeling tonight? In the zone?" JP could hear the sarcasm in Lang's voice. Lang was always sarcastic. If Lang wasn't being sarcastic then something was wrong.

"I got this one, just keep people out of my crease."

Warm up continued for another five minutes and then the team skated to the bench and went back to the locker room.

"We didn't look so good last time we played Edmonton." the coach shot a look at JP, "I don't want to see the same kind of performance tonight."

The coach pointed to the pad of paper on the wall. There was a big number twelve on the pad. He didn't need to say another word.

Nearly all the players had some pregame ritual and for JP it was a meditative time. Often he would pick a corner of the room and go through various moves and positions, defending against an imaginary opponent. It helped him focus.

Fifteen minutes later the puck dropped at center ice, the clock began ticking down, and JP felt a familiar feeling creep into his mind. The Zone. The play on the ice slowed down. He watched the puck come flying in from his left side and he easily deflected it to the corner. He caught the rebound shot with his glove hand. He heard the sound of the crowd cheering somewhere in the distance. He watched the following faceoff and faced puck after puck, a total of forty-three shots. Nothing got passed JP that night. The game ended 3-0.

After JP got home he called his brother Remy.

"Tell me a story, Remy," JP did this from time to time, called his brother and asked him to tell him a story, usually after hockey games. Remy had been telling JP stories since he was a small boy.

Remy told JP a story about a young man who took about twenty Datura seeds and had a wild hallucinogenic adventure that nearly killed him. He blacked out and had woken two days later, many miles from home, naked and covered with scratches and bruises. He had no idea how he got there. Remy was working on a book about the proper use of Datura in shamanistic practice.

The two talked for a half hour about Remy's latest work. Eventually the conversation got around to the game.

"I watched the game tonight," said Remy, "Wow, were you in the zone, or what? Nice shutout!"

The two talked for a while about the game, what it was like being in the zone, Paige's sudden departure, and about dragons.

-20-
THE PSYCHIC

The expedition didn't leave for Alaska for another ten days. Newsome had gotten the idea in his head to try and get a reporter from CNN, a certain Ms. April Matthews, to join the team. Newsome had a crush on April Matthews. Stacy had noticed the look in Newsome's eyes when he watched Ms. Matthews on the TV and wasn't going to put up with those looks while on the expedition. Stacy threatened to quit the team if April came on board. The whole incident took a week to play out.

Meanwhile, Paige had rocketed to Colorado in a two day frenzy of driving. Bessie was more than up to the challenge. She had the address for the KnewSomeMore Ltd. office buildings. She was going to start there and not give up until she met Newsome Whitmore and convinced him that she should be part of the expedition. She had a plan.

Paige was surprised when a man she recognized as Newsome was walking through the parking lot of the office building flanked by two men in dark suits. She jumped out of Bessie, followed closely by Rufus and ran up to Newsome.

"You are Newsome Whitmore and you're going to find a dragon."

Newsome was taken aback by Paige's straightforwardness, but he put up his hand to stop the two men from intervening. When Paige was on a manic she was an unstoppable force.

"And who are you?" asked Newsome, noting that Paige was easy on the eyes.

"I'm Paige Turner and I'm going to be the psychic on your expedition."

"You are?" Newsome was pleasantly amused.

"Yes, and together we're going to find a grand dragon which will make you world famous."

"I'm already world famous."

"Even more world famous-i-er," Paige smiled.

Paige rested her hand on Newsome's arm and smiled in such a way as she spoke that Newsome couldn't help but want to have Paige along on the expedition. He was in the middle of the incident with April and Stacy, and Paige seemed like a nice distraction, plus, the expedition needed a psychic. He couldn't believe he hadn't thought of that before.

Most of the rest of the team readily accepted Paige into the crew. Paige got a polo shirt with the expedition logo, a sweatshirt, an arctic jacket, and a folder of briefing information. Stacy, of course, was the only one who had reservations about Paige joining the team.

Paige had psychic blood in her family, on her mother's side, but Paige had never explored that part of herself much. Neither had Paige ever tried to pretend she was a psychic before, but now that she had put on that guise, her latent psychic abilities began to kick into action. Paige played the part of a mystic quite well, she was certainly dressed for the role. Her first prediction was that the team would be successful, and everyone liked the sound of that.

-21-
DON AND MIKE

Bud Henry was busy working on improving the designs for the trash hauling ship he was having built. He had asked his son Don to help him out but Don said he was busy. So now Mike, his older son, was hanging out with him and Hugo, helping with the designs. Bud had noticed that Don lacked enthusiasm for the project and it bothered him.

Mike was incredibly enthusiastic about the project. He was motivated by his belief in reincarnation. He figured if he was coming back again he should leave the planet a better place than he found it. He worked with his father and Hugo nearly every day to make progress on the plans. Mike loved his father, and considered himself fortunate when he thought about his place in the world. He felt sorry for Don, because, in his opinion, Don was missing out on all the fun.

Don was sulking and avoiding the project. He hated the whole ocean cleanup idea and wished he could think of a way for it to fail. Right now, all he could think of was stalling tactics. He practiced being as uncooperative as possible, without too being obvious. Meanwhile, he took legal courses online and worked towards becoming a paralegal. As a paralegal he could show his dad how much he wanted to be a lawyer, and hopefully get his dad's blessing to go into a legal career.

Bud had no idea his son really wanted to be a lawyer, or he would have told him to go ahead. Don had mentioned it a few times, but Bud didn't think he was serious. Bud stayed immersed in the plans for the project, enjoyed the time he spent with Mike and was continuously puzzled by Don's attitude.

It was mid-spring before the new version of the trash hauling ship was ready to be tested. Another test was arranged for a week later.

Deep in the Pacific Ocean, Malthusius and his castle had settled back to the bottom of a deep undersea canyon. The raising and the lowering of the island had worked exactly as Malthusius had planned. The island had been raised by Malthusius' mental control over the castle and the surrounding rocks. He was testing his vast mental powers again, flexing his mental muscles.

The four crew members from Newsome Whitmore's yacht which Malthusius had eaten recently were merely a snack and they had whetted his appetite for more humans. Humans were tasty little munchies he had discovered. He thought about the seven billion humans on the planet and the thought made him hungry. Soon, if everything went correctly, and why shouldn't it – he would have a nearly endless supply of humans to snack on. In the meantime Malthusius would get by on a diet of Kraken, whales, sharks and fish – like the occasional sea trout. Trout is a well-known fresh water fish, but there is a species of trout that live in the ocean. They are called sea trout, or sometimes *Salmo trutta*.

-22-
TROUT GOLD

Celestial Knight kept an eye on Jonas' cabin while he was gone. She watered his crops, stocked his firewood and pantry, and spent this particular late spring day hanging out on his porch, smoking a joint of JK Special. Celeste missed her brother but she figured he'd be back. He always came back.

Jonas had been off on other adventures in the past and sometimes he would share details about what he did or saw. Once he took a camera with him on his travels. He took pictures of a statue of a stallion. The statue was at the center of a park in a traffic circle. The sky was a bruised red and blue color. The stallion was rearing up on its hind legs. The statue was massive and made of gold. Jonas had said the photos were taken in the year 6713, a particularly significant year.

Some people might call Jonas a wizard, some might call him a shaman. Jonas didn't call himself anything but a simple human being, which he considered the best thing to be. Even though Jonas was born just a few years after his sister Celeste, he had lived thousands of years longer by traveling to strange and unusual planes of existence.

In this book we'll call Jonas both a wizard and a shaman. He was a mystic and a traveler of the cosmic light beam. He knew many of the secrets of eternal life and had traveled to distant galaxies. He had dined with Pleiadians and with the Nommos of Sirius. Jonas had traveled in the fifth dimension of cosmic reality, and he had traveled in the sub-dimensions where everything is a strange oozing muck of life and death.

Lately, Jonas had been off on business in another galaxy, one that exists in an unusual fold in space and time. Jonas was glad that Nathan the dragon had joined him. Jonas' plans required a dragon to succeed, and in the past he really had no idea where to get one. That was before the little tiny dragons had shown up at his window. Now that Nathan had grown a bit it was time to get down to business.

The galaxy Jonas and Nathan were visiting is barely visible from Earth using incredibly high powered space telescopes. They were on a planet, called PuloPulo by the natives, which looked like Earth in a solar system that looked a lot like ours. There was something one might call a quantum entanglement between the two solar systems.

Jonas and Nathan were wandering through a forest, in a valley. If it were on planet Earth you would swear you were walking through the Los Angeles basin, except without all the signs of civilization. Jonas was looking for a certain kind of gold, a very rare gold. Only a dragon could find this rare yellow metal. Well, anyone could find it, but dragons were the only ones who could smell the gold like a dog hunting a bone. There were several places on this planet that had deposits of the rare metal and according to the Akashic Records, the forest was one of those few places. The natives had no use for this special metal Jonas was looking for and had no objections to him mining a little to take back home. Ownership was an unknown concept to the natives of PuloPulo.

There were several native groups that lived in what we would call North America. They called the land they lived on Turtle Island and said it was once a turtle that lived under the seas, but years ago the turtle had risen up out of the sea. When the turtle rose out of the sea it turned into dry land, fields, mountains, streams, rivers and lakes. The rains came and watered the land and people grew like flowers in the fields until they were ripe and ready to be harvested. Then people climbed down from the plants where they had grown and started to walk around. This is still how people are born on this planet. The natives took Jonas out into the fields where new baby plants were just beginning to grow. The baby plants were being attended to by nurses and midwives.

The forest in the area that looked like the Los Angeles basin was dense with trees. The trees had flowers and in those flowers grew baby birds. There was an ocean to the southwest and mountains ringing the basin on three sides. Nathan was threading his way among the trees with his nose to the ground. Jonas was following right behind him. They came to a stream and Nathan paused on the bank. He scanned the surface of the water, reached into it with his snout. In a moment he resurfaced with a gold nugget in his teeth. He set the gold nugget at Jonas' feet and retrieved a second. Jonas picked up the gold nuggets and squeezed them with his fist. The nuggets were barely pliable, they weren't the rare gold Jonas was looking for on PuloPulo. Jonas thanked Nathan for finding the nuggets and they crossed the stream to continue their search.

The rare gold Jonas was looking for was soft and malleable. It would have been like soft clay in his hands when he squeezed it. The natives called it Trout Gold because it was the same color as their most abundant fish. Jonas needed the Trout Gold for a device he was working on to shield the mind from dangerous incoming telepathic messages. His crystal ball had shown him he was going to need this in the near future. He had gotten the plans for the mind shield from the Akashic Records. At this point Jonas' mind shield was in seventy-six pieces on his work bench in his garage, about a dozen feet from where his sister was sitting on the porch, smoking a joint of JK Special.

-23-
CATCH AND RELEASE

att Paulson, the artillery expert, had just come upstairs from the Tiki Lounge, which was the name of the hotel bar. The hotel was called The Springs Hotel in Colorado Springs. Matt was twenty-eight and was on the expedition because Dave Kingsley, the reality-TV star, had recommended him to Newsome Whitmore.

Dave had affectionately taken Matt under his wing and used him in several episodes of his popular hunting reality TV show, *BIG GAME: Catch and Release*. *Catch and Release* had become a whole industry unto itself and had several spin-offs including *ROD AND REEL: Catch and Release* and *FALCON HUNT: Catch and Release*.

Matt had been a hunter since he was a child. His father had tutored Matt on nearly every kind of firearm he could get his hands on. Matt had gone into the Army the week after his eighteenth birthday. Over the next six years Matt had become a munitions expert and an authority on military firepower. Not only that, but Matt had a natural gift for directions and cartography.

Dave had met Matt several years back at a party thrown by Matt's parents in Newport Beach. Matt's father had been an executive producer on Dave Kingsley's previous show, *BULLETS AND CROSSHAIRS*. *BULLETS* had been very popular in 2014-2015, but the audience quickly fell off after an episode about hunting elephants for their tusks. There was a huge internet backlash against the show, as you can expect, and a season later Dave Kingsley had been made-over as the *catch-and-release* guy.

Dave was strongly attracted to Matt, even though he had no idea he was gay. Dave was proudly heterosexual. He slept with lots of women to prove it. Matt had no idea that Dave was attracted to him, but then again, he never stopped to wonder why a star like Dave would always want to spend time with him.

Matt had his eye on Barbara Clarence, the fantasy writer with long brown hair and a sultry look. He had read seven of her novels, including her two most popular books, *Dragons of the Sun* and *The Ice Dragon*, as well as a handful of her lesser known novels like *Dragons of the Vanishing Lakes* and *I Dream of Dragons*. He had seen her on TV a few times and was quite taken with her, even though she was sixteen years older.

Barbara was living a dream. She couldn't believe she was actually on an expedition to hunt for dragons. It was like one of her books coming to life. She was looking at herself in the full length mirror. She thought she looked pretty good in her *Expedition: Dragon Hunt* sweatshirt.

Spread out on the bed were notes, photographs of Emily's dragons, several changes of clothes, an empty potato chip bag, a half empty bag of cookies, her purse, a backpack and her laptop. Barbara had been living in this room for nearly two weeks and couldn't wait to get to Alaska.

Barbara had been watching a hockey game on the TV. It was a playoff game, the Anaheim Ducks were playing the Edmonton

Oilers. The Ducks were winning 4-2. It was late in the third period. Barbara changed the channel. An episode of *BIG GAME: Catch and Release* was on. Barbara paused.

Hmmm. Dave Kingsley, she thought to herself. In any one of her books, a character like her would have a romantic interlude with Dave Kingsley's character on an expedition such as this... she let her mind drift on that thought. She picked up her notes and jotted down a few ideas her for next novel. The ideas had to do with a love scene between her story's heroine and a character that looked a lot like Dave Kingsley.

-24-
WAITING TO EXPLORE

George Marks, the adventurer extraordinaire, and Mike Kleason, the diver, had been friends for nearly forty years. They had worked on projects in the past and were glad to be on another adventure together. Their wives had been roommates in college, and that's how they had met, on double dates. Over the years their two families had combined vacations on at least a half dozen occasions. Now all the kids had grown and left the nest.

Mike was going to retire as a professional diver after this expedition. He had no idea why Newsome had invited him to join the team, but he was glad for one last paycheck before retirement. KnewSomeMore Ltd. had offered him $100,000 to join the team for two weeks. Now, because of the delays, they were going to pay him another $100,000.

George had convinced Newsome to hire Mike. George had been the second person Newsome had hired for the expedition. Marks had been to numerous remote locations around the world and was author to a highly-cited series of travel books, called *Marks The Spot*. He was the only person in the world to both climb Mount Everest and travel to the bottom of the Mariana Trench.

You can recount his adventures in his popular book, *My Earth, From Top To Bottom*. It's quite a read.

George and Mike had adjoining hotel rooms and liked to keep the door open between their rooms. They had watched a hockey game together, the same one that Barbara had been watching. The Ducks had won 5-2 and were up two games to none in the series. Now they changed the channel and started watching a new special on the Discovery channel called *Dragons: A History.* Barbara Clarence was one of the people interviewed for the special.

Down in the Tiki Lounge, Dave Kingsley was having drinks with Emily Lafleur and Paige Turner. Paige had left Rufus in her hotel room, stretched out on the king size bed. Emily and Paige had been having a nice time getting to know each other before Dave had joined them. Now the conversation revolved around the world of Dave. Dave was pretty sure that Paige was going to be an easy catch in his ongoing effort to prove his heterosexuality. Paige, of course, was in pursuit of Newsome and flatly rebuffed all of Dave's advances. Emily watched Dave pursue Paige and found it amusing.

On the other side of Colorado Springs, Stacy Barnett was making love to Newsome Whitmore. Newsome had agreed not to invite Ms. April Matthews along on the expedition and Stacy was feeling like she had won this round. Stacy had that stance in the world. It was Stacy versus everyone else in an endless game of competition.

Newsome had no idea of the games going on in Stacy's head, all he thought about was the dragons. Well, that's not all he thought about. He thought about the beast with the huge tentacles that had eaten his crew members on his last expedition. The creature haunted him day and night, especially at night in his dreams. The monster visited him often in his dreams, it was like the monster knew where to find him. Newsome was also haunted by the loss of four crew members on his last expedition, he hoped he wouldn't lose any of his team this time around.

Far to the north Alexander was falling asleep in his cave. He had eaten a fine meal of roasted deer, and he had pleasant thoughts in his head. Then a different sound intruded on his thoughts. He knew it was a song, even though he had never heard a song before. He turned his ears towards the sound, but it came from inside of him. He let out a puzzled puff of smoke. The song made him uncomfortable and he tried to block out the sound. Happily, he discovered that when he tried to block out the sound it worked. In a few moments his mind was quiet and he went back to thinking about the roasted deer and other pleasant thoughts.

-25-
A LAWYER?

The house of Malthusius was two hundred feet tall and had thousands of square feet of space. It was a castle anchored to a huge, flat rock that rested on the bottom of the ocean in a canyon covered by a forest of seaweed. The walls of the castle were built of solid granite and coral and weighed thousands of tons. The castle was built in a bygone age, and the walls were infused with magic. The structure barely contained Malthusius as he sat upon his massive throne in the main hall of the great stone house. The granite helped to amplify his mental signals to the outside world. There was no roof on his castle.

On the great throne Malthusius sat and pondered his plans. He sang his songs and listened to the world of humans through his psychic senses. Everything was going perfectly. His subtle songs had reached their target audience. Slowly the human race was getting used to hearing his songs. One doesn't want too move to fast and startle their prey. Soon the humans would be lining up to be eaten, but that was a step or two down the road.

Malthusius had found thousands of humans as receptive as Hugo Branson. Slowly he was taking over their minds. Malthusius had learned a lot of details about the current state of the world from reading the minds of these humans. He had no respect for the conventions of human beings, the building of empires and the triumphs and travails of nations. Soon he would remake the world according to his own plans, but first he wanted the humans to clean up the messes they had made. Mostly he wanted his ocean cleaned up.

Bud Henry was busy doing just what Malthusius wanted. He was planning the first of the ocean cleanup voyages. Trash collects in two main patches in the Pacific Ocean, and one of the patches was relatively close to the West Coast. A majority of the visible trash was plastic: lids, bottles, wrappings, six-pack holders, bags, straws, and other various pieces of plastic. And cigarette butts. There were an endless amount of cigarette butts floating among the trash. The trash covered an area of approximately 680,000 square miles, or more than twice the size of Texas. Bud's goal was to reduce that area down to nothing over the next ten years. It was an ambitious goal.

Melissa's online funding campaign was still bringing in lots of money. Recently both Google and Amazon had gotten on board with huge grants towards the project. *National Geographic* was almost done with the first part of the series they were producing on the clean up. Bud's trash skimmer and garbage collection ship had both passed their tests, and Bud was able to get a big loan and some financing from the National Oceanic and Atmospheric Administration to start building a small fleet of ships. They would be ready to go by late summer. The ship building companies were working around the clock to get the fleet ready.

One night Don Henry had decided to talk to his sister Melissa about his ambition to be a lawyer. Don had been visiting Melissa and her husband Harlan and the evening had included dinner and more then a few beers. The beers had loosened Don's lips and he ended up telling Melissa and Harlan how much he hated the ocean clean-up project.

Melissa had been taken aback by how much Don talked down the project. She tried reasoning with him, but eventually she started to listen to what he had to say.

"I want to be a lawyer, Melissa," Don said earnestly.

"A lawyer? Why?" Melissa was seriously confused by Don's ambitions.

"It's been my dream since I was a kid. Remember watching re-runs of *Perry Mason* on TV?"

Melissa had hated *Perry Mason*, but she kept quiet about that.

"You know being a lawyer isn't anything like *Perry Mason*, right?" asked Melissa.

"Oh, I know."

"So, you want to help fight for justice?"

"No, I want to be a corporate lawyer, maybe for a big oil company. Everyone cares so much about the ocean and it makes me sick. I like cars, electricity and warm homes. I couldn't give a crap about the supposed 'climate change' bullshit. I think the whole climate change thing is a big con job. The oil companies have helped make our civilization what it is, the height of human achievement."

Melissa was thrown off by this. She hadn't expected this from her younger brother. She believed the complete opposite of what Don was expressing.

"Oh," said Melissa. She looked at Harlan for help.

"Have you talked to Bud about this lawyer thing?" asked Harlan.

"Yeah, but the old man never listens."

"I'll talk to him," offered Melissa. She wanted to get Don off the project now that he had revealed his true feelings.

"Would you? I'd really appreciate it."

"Sure, no problem."

Melissa talked to her father about it the next morning.

"A lawyer? How about that..." Bud vaguely remembered Don mentioning it once or twice.

Bud called up his son that afternoon and fired him from the salvage crew. Bud told his son he better go back to school if he wanted to become a lawyer, and offered to pay for the whole thing.

It was the best day of Don Henry's young life.

-26-
THAT SONG

The second series of the playoffs for the Anaheim Ducks was going their way and after four games they were up three to one. Edmonton was on the brink of elimination, and the next game was going to be at the Honda Center. In the locker room a pad of paper hung on the wall and it had a big number nine written on the top sheet. JP had an astounding 2.13 goals-against average and was trying not to think about those kind of numbers. There would be an off season to think about statistics, but for now JP was staying focused on the task at hand.

JP was working with his goaltending coach. The coach had noticed a couple areas where JP was getting sloppy and wanted to tighten up those areas of his game. They were running through a bunch of drills to remind JP to focus on the fundamentals: stick on the ice, square to the shooter, keeping his goal pads tight against the goal posts. And then skating drills. JP was one of the best skaters on the team, and could scramble on the ice and regain his position in seconds. The coach wanted him to be even quicker. After two hours of hard practice JP hit the showers.

Lang Nichols and his wife Svetlana had invited JP over for dinner. Lang lived with his wife in the Anaheim Hills. They had two small children, both girls. A decade ago Lang had played for a year in Russia where he had met Svetlana. Now Lang was a veteran in the NHL at thirty-two years old.

From Lang's backyard you could see across Orange County, and on a clear day you could see the Pacific Ocean in the distance. JP and Lang were standing in the backyard by the pool having an ice cold beer. After a bit of small talk JP brought up something that had been weighing on his mind.

"I've been hearing a song in my head that just won't go away."

The song had been on his mind a lot and was really distracting, in a relaxing way. He needed to talk to someone about it.

"You do? What kind of song?" Lang asked, surprisingly unsarcastic.

"I don't know. Kind of hard to describe. It sounds far away. Sometimes it fades in and out. When I'm concentrated on the game or in the zone I don't hear it."

"Is it a low and melancholy sound?"

"You could call it that but it doesn't make me feel sad, just the opposite. It's quite relaxing, actually."

"It's a strange song... glad you brought this up. I've been hearing a song too, it must be the same one," said Lang. He was feeling relieved, maybe he wasn't going crazy like he had been thinking. Dementia ran in Lang's family and he had been worried that he might be losing his mind. He was so worried he hadn't even mentioned it to Svetlana. Svetlana, unbeknownst to Lang, was also hearing the song.

Lang wasn't the only person wondering about their sanity. Der had flown back to Oregon and the song was playing constantly in his mind, and that was causing him to worry. His mind had run through several scenarios about his mental state that all involved him going insane and ending up homeless. In spite of his worries, Der really liked the song, it was rather catchy and made him want to draw.

Der was back to his work routine. Der was a web designer and built websites for artists, writers, design firms, architects, everything from small sites to large e-commerce solutions. He usually juggled four or five clients per month and helped maintain over a dozen different websites for ongoing accounts. Der kept busy and was well loved by his clients.

In the evenings, after business was done for the day, Der spent his time drawing. All his worries went away when he drew. Mostly he liked to draw erotic pictures of men. He had a whole series he had drawn of Paul LePaul, both with and without his elegant gowns.

Now, because of the song, Der was drawing cephalopods. He had pages of sketches in his latest notebook of close-up drawings of huge tentacles. Drawing the large suckers on the tentacles had become an obsession. Der would take hits of pot, listen to the song in his head and draw into the early morning hours.

One morning Der taped a number of the drawings onto his sliding closet doors like puzzle pieces, and the collected drawings had started to form the image of a gigantic beast. Der took the day off from work, smoked pot all day, listened to the song in his head and drew pictures of the beast on his closet doors. It was like a massive octopus or a giant squid, but something was different and monstrous about this creature, something strangely intelligent. Der called the creature Malthusius. It was the name that was in his mind.

Der wasn't the only one making drawings and sculptures of the strange cephalopod creature. Bernard Engels, a renowned English artist had begun work on a new sculpture, chiseling away at a large piece of marble over twelve feet tall. He had been interviewed by

The Guardian newspaper about his latest work and this is what he had said about the piece:

"I'm looking for the cephalopod inside the marble, the Master of the Earth."

Hardly anyone paid attention to what Bernard Engels had said, except for one impressionable artist out in Joshua Tree, California, Wolf Thomas. He was a big fan of Bernard Engels' work. He had read the interview online.

Wolf not only heard the song but also had visions of the giant cephalopod called Malthusius. He knew that Malthusius was Master or Lord of the Earth. Wolf was silently saying prayers all day long to Malthusius. He had built an altar and was burning candles daily.

Wolf was a painter and was painting a number of canvases related to his new God. Wolf knew several other people who were blessed enough to hear the same song in their heads and together they formed a small religion. The religion called itself the Church of Malthusius.

-27-
THE CHURCH OF MALTHUSIUS

The Church of Malthusius in Joshua Tree was not the only Church of Malthusius in the world. There were, at the time of Wolf Thomas' epiphany about Malthusius and his lordship, 327 different, small groups that worshiped the great cephalopod in various ways. In Malaysia there were several groups that incorporated human sacrifice into their Church's practices. Deep in Louisiana, a large congregation had given themselves over to being possessed by Malthusius. They had large orgies deep in the swamps of cephalopodic ecstasy. On an island in the Pacific a group of worshipers chose to give their lives to their Lord and Master and took to throwing themselves into the ocean in hopes of being eaten by their Lord.

Malthusius smiled to himself, if a cephalopod can be said to smile. All this worship made him feel like traveling and having himself a snack of these Pacific Islanders. He left his castle behind and traveled across the ocean to the particular island with the native worshipers. As Malthusius neared the shore of the island he began to rise up out of the water. He sang a calling song.

The natives of the island came to a cliff overlooking the ocean, drawn by the song of their Lord and Master. They bowed down on the cliff. They chanted songs of praise to Malthusius. Some of the natives got up and ran to the edge of the cliff and threw themselves over in an attempt to get closer to their Master. Malthusius stood in the water, fifty feet tall, and caught the various natives as they jumped off the cliff. More than a dozen natives became a nice meal for Malthusius. *This is the life*, thought Malthusius.

No one heard about the natives in the Pacific, or about the various Churches of Malthusius. It wasn't on social media, it wasn't in the papers and even though there were websites for the churches popping up, no one was going to them. All of it was going on in the background of life.

Around the world a good thirty percent of the population was now listening to the song of Malthusius, and the effect of this had deeply permeated the fabric of society. There was a hypnotic mellowness which settled across the world. Everywhere people were being kinder to each other. As I mentioned earlier, due to some kind of social cooperation that no one could have planned or implemented, nearly all the traffic jams of the world had disappeared. Traffic moved seamlessly and effortlessly throughout the world. It was hard to complain about the subtle changes going on.

Now Malthusius had a new song to sing. It was much like the last one but more intense. It was meant to reach half the population of humans, or more.

-28-

THE SONG HEARD AROUND THE WORLD

L il' Billy followed up the success of "Ocean" with a cover of "Sailing", a song made popular by Christopher Cross, which earned three Grammy Awards in 1979. The original song was written by Carter Burwell, an America film composer who frequently worked with the Coen Brothers.

Lil' Billy and his producers were on a hot streak with two hits already from his album *Dreamsongs*. There were plans being made for a big tour that fall. Lil' Billy and his crew were going to open for Miley Cyrus. There was talk of having Christopher Cross joining the tour for a handful of dates to sing "Sailing" with Lil' Billy. These were heady times. Lil' Billy was drinking a fifth of Jack Daniels Old No. 7 whiskey a day and had been introduced to the world of heroin and cocaine. Unfortunately, these were bad drugs for a reckless and cocky son-of-a-bitch like Lil' Billy.

Lil' Billy didn't survive the month of May. He died on Memorial Day while partying in his hot tub. He was dead before the ambulance arrived. His consciousness had pushed off from the sphere of the living, looked back and gave the world the finger before he disappeared into a tunnel of light. No one was surprised when the cause of death was announced as an overdose from an excessive amounts of alcohol, cocaine and heroin.

JP was bummed out by the news of Lil' Billy's death. He heard about the death while watching the news, sitting alone in his rented house in Yorba Linda. It was Memorial Day, late in the evening, and the Anaheim Ducks were on a break between series in the playoffs. They had eliminated the Edmonton Oilers in five games and were waiting to find out who their next opponent was going to be, the Los Angeles Kings or Detroit Red Wings.

After watching the news he called his brother Remy, but Remy didn't answer. He left a message for Remy to call back if he felt like it. He put on Lil' Billy's hit song "Ocean", the extended mix, and decided to cook a late night steak with some french fries. He got a beer out of the fridge and opened it. He put the french fries in the oven. He looked at his social media news feed on his phone. News of Lil' Billy's death was all over the feed.

JP sat at the counter, drinking his beer and feeling sad when the song of Malthusius started to fade into his mind once "Ocean" came to an end. It took his mind off of Lil' Billy and made him feel relaxed. Incredibly relaxed. He had heard the song before, but now it was much more intense. JP's mind became a flow of ideas as it loosened up from the sadness that had settled on him from the news about Lil' Billy. He decided to re-watch the game he had lost against Edmonton. It had only been a week ago but it was starting to fade from his memory.

JP sat on the sofa and ate his steak and fries watching the first period of the game. Edmonton had scored twice during that period. JP watched both goals several times in slow motion. Once the puck had been deflected just past his glove hand and one goal came when the puck squeezed between his pads and the goal post. His goaltending coach had not been happy about that goal and that had been the reason for the special goaltending practice covering the fundamentals.

JP fell asleep on the sofa after the steak dinner. Remy's phone call woke him around two in the morning. Remy was baking on magic mushrooms, which was pretty normal for Remy.

"Tell me a story, Remy," said JP, his mind still full of the cobwebs of his dreams.

Remy told JP a tale that Sam, the little green magic mushroom elf, had told him that evening. It was full of unusual colors, extreme angles and the story had no plot at all. Somewhere in the story sublime philosophical truths were revealed. These truths were lost on JP as he sat listening to Remy's fantastical elf story, which was blended with a recounting of the evening's mushroom inspired adventures.

"...and then I called you," Remy ended his story.

"Lil' Billy died today," said JP, a little more awake now.

"No, you're shitting me."

"Yeah. Probably an overdose. He died in his hot tub in the middle of a big party. Freaked everyone out... he died before the ambulance arrived. He was the same age I am."

"Stay away from drugs," responded Remy, without a trace of irony, "what are you doing tomorrow?"

"I have practice. We're getting ready for the next series. Why do you ask?"

"Just wondered if you wanted to come out to the desert for a few days."

"I can't, I hope to be busy until the middle of June with the playoffs."

"Well, after you win the Stanley Cup bring it out to the desert and we'll throw a huge party."

The brothers talked a bit more. When the call ended JP checked his social media news feed again. He scrolled through the various stories and nothing caught his eye until he saw a post his brother had shared earlier that evening. The post was about a person hearing a song in their head that wouldn't go away.

The shared post had thousands of likes and hundreds of comments. Apparently a lot of people had been hearing the same song in their head, and strangely, no one had been talking about it yet. The person who had written the original post was a social media friend of Remy's in Joshua Tree, a girl named Cassie Stackwell. Cassie's post broke the dam of silence about the song, and the next day the song being heard around the world was the topic on everyone's mind.

-29-
DRAGONS FOR REAL

Newsome Whitmore and *Expedition: Dragon Hunt* headed for Alaska after Memorial Day. The team settled in the Hotel Alaskan, occupying the entire second floor, including a large conference room. The conference room became the expedition's base of operations. A giant *Expedition: Dragon Hunt* banner was strung across one end of the conference room, and there were tables arranged in a large U shape with chairs all around the outside of the tables. A small collection of whiteboards and a video monitor were set up at the opening of the U.

It was the first of June when the whole team finally assembled in the conference room to really begin the expedition. Paige smudged the room with sage and said a pantheistic prayer for safety and success. She placed a small collection of crystals, bought in Colorado Springs, on the floor in the middle of the U. Paige was wearing a flowing dress and several scarves. Her performance looked convincingly mystical and psychic, which was what Paige had intended.

Newsome began the meeting with a video presentation covering the major points of the expedition. The presentation showed

the glaciers and the mountain they would be exploring. It included a section by Barbara Clarence, the author, about the various kinds of dragons and their nature and abilities. Barbara's information was based on fiction, of course, and turned out to be worthless when it was really needed.

After the video presentation Matt Paulson, the navigation and artillery expert, got up and handed a packet of maps to each team member. He proceeded to explain the maps while also explaining some of firepower available to the team. Dave Kingsley, realizing this wasn't going to be like his reality TV show, got up next to explain the preliminary plans to capture a dragon, involving large steel cables and several helicopters. He was faking it because he was in over his head with no idea what to do. He also felt like it was too late to back out.

Mike Kleason, the diver and biologist, talked for a bit about the Hubbard glacier and the possible marine diet of the dragons. Mike, unfortunately, was truly boring whenever he spoke in front of people and almost put the team to sleep. George Marks, the renowned adventurer, woke everyone back up with his exciting tales of various expeditions he had been on over the years. After George Marks was done talking everyone was feeling excited about the expedition.

The next day the team boarded a ship to travel to the glacier. The group planned be at sea for the next five days. Everyone wore their brand new *Expedition: Dragon Hunt* arctic jackets. Newsome was feeling an intense excitement. Somewhere deep inside himself he knew that this whole expedition was going to succeed, like Paige had predicted. He looked around the ship and was proud of the team he had assembled – *history is being written in this very moment*, he thought.

The ship they were on was the *Arctic Sea Skipper II*, a fifty-five foot cruiser owned by KnewSomeMore Ltd. The first mate was Gustaf Johansen, the Norwegian survivor of Newsome's last expedition across the Pacific. Gustaf was a big fan of Lil' Billy and often played his album *Dreamsongs* on the bridge of the ship.

It was several hours before the ship reached the open water. First the ship sailed through a number of inlets and passed several islands on its way to the ocean. Once they reached the ocean it was calm and inviting. The days were long and the weather was beautiful in early June, a relaxed vibe settled over the whole team. Paige did a tarot card reading after dinner and declared tomorrow to be a special day of new beginnings.

On the second day out of port they neared the Hubbard Glacier. Emily happened to be filming off the side of the ship that morning when a thunder of dragons was sighted in the distance. They were flying in the direction of the ship before they disappeared into the ocean a hundred yards away. Someone yelled "dragons!" and everyone gathered on deck immediately.

Suddenly, several dragons came bursting out of the water just dozens of yards from the ship. A large wave rocked the *Arctic Sea Skipper II*. The thunderous sound of dragon wings flapping filled the air. One of the dragons had a young killer whale in its claws and the dragon flipped the whale high into the sky. Fire shot from the dragon's mouth and the now fried whale fell back towards the sea only to be caught by a second dragon. The dragons dove back into the ocean with their prey. Several more dragons flew out of the water, hovered in the air a hundred feet above the ship and then dove back into the waves.

Finally, a ways off, the thunder of dragons flew up from the water and took to the sky. The expedition team watched the dragons disappear somewhere beyond the glaciers.

The team was out of their minds about the dragon sighting. This was even better than they had expected. Newsome had taken some detailed photos of the dragons with his digital SLR and

Emily had caught some amazing footage. Everyone on the team had seen the dragons up close. Now there was a reality to the expedition that hadn't existed before. Dragons were real.

-30-
BECOMING MALTHUSIUSIAN

Wolf Thomas had reinvented himself over the last month. His previous life as a hi-desert artist took a backseat to his new-found religion. The Church of Malthusius in Joshua Tree had grown to include a dozen like-minded individuals. Wolf had built a shrine to Malthusius on his land. His friend and fellow church member, Dave "The Bear" Williams had constructed a large statue made of recyclable trash, resembling a massive cephalopod on a throne. The church members gathered several times a day to bow down to the image of Malthusius.

The members also spent hours meditating and listening to the songs of Malthusius. They had discovered that smoking pot made the song stronger, so they started to smoke lots of marijuana. Every few days someone new would show up at Wolf Thomas' five acres of land, ready to join the Church. The new people seemed to know where to show up.

Soon, word started to get around Joshua Tree that a group of individuals were gathering together to listen to the song folks were hearing in their heads. Many people, especially creative types and pot smokers, were hearing the song of Malthusius strongly and were curious about what they were hearing. In the hi-desert the population was overwhelmingly slanted toward creative types and pot smokers, so many people hoped the Church might have some kind of answers.

The Church of Malthusius did not have any answers. Nor did they have many questions. They existed in a state of grace inspired by their new-found faith. They heard the song and the song brought peace to their anxiety-filled lives, wasn't that enough?

Of course, there were trade-offs. There was a loss of individuality that came with concentrating on the song of Malthusius. This seemed like a small price to pay for achieving such peace of mind. Among the Church members they called this transformation "becoming more Malthusiusian," and this was considered a great thing.

There were others not thrilled with the song of Malthusius. Among those displeased by the song was the Pentagon. The song tended to make the soldiers who could hear it docile and less likely to fight in their many ongoing wars around the world. It was having an effect on morale and this was unacceptable. The Pentagon was seriously looking into the situation.

Wolf Thomas, who was trying hard to become more Malthusiusian, wouldn't have appreciated the Pentagon's perspective on Malthusius. To him, becoming Malthusiusian was the end of a long spiritual journey.

Once upon a time, years earlier, when he had lived in Irvine, California his name had been Charles Thomas and he had been a financial speculator. That was before a satori moment that came along with a heart attack at the young age of thirty-three. Charles quit his profession and took up painting. Several years later he changed his first name to Wolf, which he had determined was his spirit animal, and several years after that he moved to Joshua Tree. Now he had five acres off of Sunny Vista Road that was being covered with tents as new people showed up wanting to join the quickly growing church. This was all unexpected, the church business, and Wolf hadn't figured out a long term plan, but he knew he was going to need one.

There were also small anti-cult groups formed in direct opposition to the growing number of Churches of Malthusius around the world. Jerry Jones was typical of the members of the opposition groups. Jerry was a white nationalist who lived in Idaho. The song had faded in and out of his mind for weeks and he hated it. He and his buddies talked about the hated song endlessly and vowed to resist the song and the Church of Malthusius. Consequently they hated cephalopods, intensely. The angrier they got about the song, the more they heard the song, which, of course, drove them crazy.

When news of a bombing attack at the Aquarium of Monterey, in which several octopuses were killed, reached Jerry and his buddies they thought it was the greatest thing in the world. They planned to commit a copycat crime at the Aquarium of Boise, soon. Jerry and his buddies called themselves the Anti-Cephalopod Front, or A.C.F. They laid low until the time was right to strike. Meanwhile, they collected machetes, guns and explosives and studied the layout of the Aquarium.

-31-
THE I CHING SAYS

*E*xpedition: *Dragon Hunt* posted new footage of the recent sighting of dragons on their website and on YouTube. The clips were viewed millions of times. From around the world stories were starting to surface about various dragon sightings. Wendell DuPont, a wealthy big game hunter, aware of the Newsome Whitmore expedition and jealous of Newsome's head start, claimed he was going to be the first person to put a stuffed dragon head on the wall of his great hall. He was going to China immediately where a number of dragons had been reportedly seen. As it turned out, Wendell DuPont was the first person killed by a dragon.

Wendell had no idea how immune to gunfire dragons are, for the most part. There are a few soft spots where a bullet might penetrate, but the muscles of the dragon were like steel cables and a bullet wouldn't penetrate very far.

The dragon Wendell had tried to shoot heard the sound of several bullets deflecting off of his scales, turned in the direction of where the shots had come from and let out a burst of white hot flame. Wendell was toasted beyond recognition along with six members of his hunting party.

Newsome read about Wendell's ill-fated hunting trip with great interest. Capturing a dragon without being burnt to a crisp seemed to be a bit of a problem. Newsome talked with his team and wondered if someone could come up with an idea about how to extinguish dragon flames. No one had any ideas. Paige suggested they consult the I Ching.

Paige threw the I Ching six times and got hexagram 26. This is what the I Ching said in response to the question "how do you capture a dragon?":

Ta Ch'u / Recharging Power

Heaven's motherlode waits within the Mountain: The Superior Person mines deep into history's wealth of wisdom and deeds, charging his character with timeless strength.

Persevere. Drawing sustenance from these sources creates good fortune. Then you may cross to the far shore.

Everyone pondered the words of the I Ching. "Heaven's motherlode waits within the mountain" seemed to apply to their situation. Barbara Clarence said she was going to do some more research on the history of Chinese dragons to try and find "history's wealth of wisdom and deeds". Matt Paulson was going to make maps coordinating where all the known dragon sightings took place. Matt was also going to research ways to create flame retardant shoulder launched missiles to attack a dragon if necessary.

Barbara found out from her research that according to ancient legends, the only way to kill a dragon was to shoot it with an arrow dipped in the tears of a virgin who has cried for joy. This, apparently, was the trick – *virgin joy tears*. Newsome had an ad put in the paper offering to pay a virgin a half million dollars for several pints of her tears, thinking a half million dollars should bring tears of joy to any young virgin's eyes.

Molly Pritchard was one of the first to respond to Newsome's advertisement. Molly was both a virgin and she had an eye condition that caused her eyes to tear-up constantly. She needed thousands of dollars for an operation to fix the problem. Molly was overjoyed to finally be able to get an operation to stop crying for the first time in years. The team collected several pints of virgin joy tears over several days.

Dave Kingsley was studying old videos of his reality TV show, *BIG GAME: Catch and Release*, trying to think up a strategy for the current situation. Dave had never gone after such beasts as these dragons. On his show he always had backup hunters even though they were never shown on screen. Now he was, quite frankly, scared shitless about having to face these beasts, real fire-breathing dragons. Bows and arrows just weren't his thing and he had talked to Newsome about soaking some bullets in the remaining virgin tears.

Matt visited a foundry in Juneau and had custom shells for the shoulder missile launchers filled with soda bi-carbonate and CO_2. His shells were fire extinguisher missiles. He had dozens of shells made and the tip of each one was painted with a small X of virgin tears.

Stacy Barnett and Newsome had been making daily flights around Mount St. Elias to survey the area. George Marks and Mike Kleason went along to help try and spot any places where there might be dragons. There were several caves visible from the air and once Mike thought he had seen a blue dragon in a clearing. By the time Stacy had circled the plane around, whatever-it-was had disappeared under the tree cover.

That evening in the conference room the team mapped out four possible locations to begin their search. *Heaven's motherlode waits within the mountain* had become an article of faith to the expedition. KnewSomeMore Ltd. hired a local wilderness outfitter and tour guides, a company called There and Back Explorers, to take them as close to Mount St. Elias as the known off-road trails would allow.

Hans Geller and his brother Ulrick were the owners of There and Back Explorers. Their family had lived in the area for three generations and the brothers knew the back country better than anyone. The Geller brothers hired a bunch of porters to haul the team's gear with Jeeps and ATVs deep into the back country. It was the seventh of June when *Expedition: Dragon Hunt* headed out in a convoy from Juneau to Mount St. Elias. The team's spirits were high as they set out. Paige and Rufus sat in the back seat of the second Jeep in the convoy, driven by Dave Kingsley. Paige had done another tarot card reading for the expedition before they left and had announced that finding a dragon was in the near future for the expedition.

Matt Paulson sat in the passenger seat and Dave slapped Matt playfully on the knee as they pulled out from the hotel parking lot.

"Here we go," said Dave Kingsley, smiling to hide his fear.

Matt smiled back, "Let's go catch a dragon."

-32-
CONFERENCE FINALS

J P stood in a corner of the locker room. He went through his various moves, defending against an imaginary opponent. Lang was moving from player to player making a number of sarcastic remarks. It was Lang's thing to do before each game. Being the team captain Lang liked to check in with each of his team mates before they headed out to the ice.

The coach had conversations with a few different players and his assistant coaches. Then he addressed the team.

"You know what kind of team the Kings are and you know the history of our team's rivalry. I want you to keep your emotions in check and don't take any bad penalties. I want you to attack the goal hard and fast. Their goaltender is the best in the league and we need to solve him fast. Shoot to his upper glove side. Watch out for the neutral zone trap. The Kings are going to clog up the middle of the ice and cut off your passing lanes. I want quick, short passes," the coach shot a look in the direction of Lang. Lang loved the big outlet pass and the fast breakaway.

The coach was really worried about the series ahead. He had hoped Detroit would have beaten Los Angeles. The Ducks style of

hard, fast hockey worked well against Detroit, but the Kings played a slower kind of hockey, a more cautious game. Their coach had been a defenseman in the league for twenty years, and believed in a defensive approach. If the Kings scored first and took over the contest it was going to be a tortuously slow affair. The solution, simply put, was to score first and make the Kings play Ducks style hockey.

The tickets for the Ducks and Kings playoff series was the hottest ticket in town. This was the first time the Southern California rivals had met in the playoffs, a series being called the Freeway Faceoff. As the Duck's coach mentioned, the Kings had the hottest goaltender in the playoffs, Mats Daniels, a Montreal native. Mats had an amazing 1.76 goals against, and the Kings had a record of nine 1-0 games in the regular season. No goaltender had ever racked up as many shutouts as Mats did so quickly. Many opponents feared that if the Kings scored first the game was over.

The series between Detroit and Los Angeles had gone to seven games and the Kings had played just two days earlier. It had been over a week since the Ducks had played and a little rust had started to settle in. The coach had done his best to keep the team fresh, but practice, even a hard practice, was no substituent for playing play-off hockey.

Before the game someone threw a dead octopus out on the ice. This was an old hockey tradition. The eight legs of the octopus represented the eight games still needed to be won to claim the Stanley Cup.

The Ducks came out flat in the first period, and the Kings scored two goals in the first five minutes. After that the pace of the game slowed down and it was a relentless crawl. The score stayed the same until late in the third period. The Ducks pulled JP from the goal and put an extra attacker on the ice. The Kings got a penalty and the Ducks ended up scoring on the power play with one minute and three seconds left in the game. The last minute was intense, and the Ducks had three prime opportunities, but failed to score.

The coach was not happy after the game. He let the team know how he felt and then reeking of disappointment he silently left the locker room. A big number eight was left hanging on the pad of paper on the locker room wall.

-33-

THE ART OF MALTHUSIUS

D er had been invited to show his many drawings of the giant cephalopod in an upcoming art show. The theme of the art show was the song everyone was hearing. The owner of the gallery was a lesbian name Delaware Evans and she titled the show "The Song of Malthusius". Der had known Delaware for several years and had built the website for her gallery, ARTWERKS on Blair, a hip gallery that showed some of the most adventurous, outsider art in southern Oregon.

Delaware, or Dela as her friends called her, was working with a book designer to put together a catalog for the show. The book designer was John Tillerman, a well-known Oregon poet. John had been having ongoing dreams about the song, dreams of giant castles underwater with a monstrous cephalopodian Lord. The dreams spanned great ages, and his dreams beheld the dreams of the cephalopod Master whose name was Malthusius. John had written a long poem about Malthusius which was going to be printed in the catalog.

John's poem began like this:

Undersea the world's Lord,

comes looking,
hunger and anger in his mind.
Human time has ended,
looking back,
relaxed and unaware in their minds.

The poem was epic in scale and foretold the end of the empires of humans as Malthusius arose from the depths to reclaim his world. No one paid any attention to John's poem, except Dela Evans. Such is the poet's fate in this age.

The poem together with Der's drawings was a prophetic statement. Everyone missed out on it. Such is the fate of prophetic statements in this age.

Also in the upcoming art show at ARTWERKS on Blair was a young sculpturer named Michael Pritchard, the brother of virgin Molly Pritchard. Michael had made a dozen small statuettes in clay of his vision of Malthusius. The sculptures were all very intricate, full of detail, between six inches and two feet tall.

Michael existed within his own world. The song was the first thing that had connected him with the world at large. Michael had schizophrenia and talked with people no one else could see. I'm not saying the people he was talking to weren't there, I'm just saying no one else could see them. No one knew how mean the people Michael listened to were. They yelled obscenities at him constantly. He did his best to ignore them but it was difficult. Working with clay was one of the few things that made these unseen people go away. When Michael worked with clay the voices were replaced by the beautiful and melancholy song so many other people were hearing. The song gave Michael visions, inescapable visions of a magnificent cephalopod, a majestic cephalopod, Malthusius, the Lord and Master of the Earth.

The art show was having its opening on the eighteenth of June and there was a lot to get done before then. Dela and John were working late hours trying to get the catalog ready in time.

This show had come together unexpectedly the month before, when the song of Malthusius burst upon the consciousness of the world. Dela was used to scheduling shows at least six months ahead of time. But then she had found out about Der's drawings at the same time she had found out about John's poem and Michael's sculptures. Dela bumped the next month's show and decided to have this show instead. Dela didn't usually work this way, but there was a kind of synchronicity going on, so she went with it. Of course, this could have been the effects of the song on her, it's hard to say.

-34-
SISSY MUSIC

Major General Merl Dawson was put in charge of solving the song of Malthusius at the Pentagon. Merl could hear the song, most of the time he was agitated by it. Merl was, by nature, adverse to relaxing. The last time he had truly relaxed was for five minutes, back in 1983. He hated soft relaxing music, sissy music he called it. Something about the song of Malthusius reminded Merl of soft relaxing music.

"Do you think this damn sissy music is a Russian trick?" Merl had asked his colleague, Lieutenant General Darrell Bowman. Darrell hated sissy music too, but he couldn't hear the song everyone was talking about.

"Hell yeah, attempting to sap the strength of our good fighting men. It pisses me off," Bowman stabbed the air with his cigar to make his point.

"We have some fine men and women working on the problem, General, the best. I hope to have some answers by next week."

"Make it happen," Bowman always liked to end a meeting with his personal catch phrase, "make it happen."

"Yes, sir." said Merl, and he gave his colleague a snappy salute.

Making it happen was exactly what Merl Dawson had in mind. He had a team of specialists from many different fields working on the problem at that very moment. The team included several physicists, a chemical engineer, an IT engineer, an astrophysicist, two sensitives or psychics who specialized in remote viewing, and three audio engineers.

The team hadn't been able to locate the source of the song, yet. It seemed to just exist, or the Earth itself was resonating with the song. Several team members wondered if the song had anything to do with the recent dragon sightings. The sensitives found all their attempts at remote viewing foiled, it was like the channel with the song was jamming their psychic abilities. The team had a number of the specialized instruments, but none of them could pick up the song. It appeared to the team that the only instrument capable of hearing the song was the human mind. They came to the conclusion that the song was some kind of psychic projection from somewhere. Where, was the question?

Malthusius could feel the psychics probing him, looking for the source of the song. It had been a simple thing to shut them down. Humans weren't capable of resisting his cephalopodian mental powers and so far he had used just a fraction of his vast mental reserves. Malthusius had no interest in being found at this moment, and a cephalopod that wants to stay hidden is a cephalopod you'll never see.

General Dawson called General Belltower, who was known to work with various extraterrestrial species, to see if he had any ideas about the song. Could it be of alien origin? General Belltower informed General Dawson that the song was, in fact, making many alien species flee the planet. Something had them spooked and there was currently a mass exodus of aliens from Earth.

"Really, just fleeing?" asked General Dawson.

"Been going on for about three weeks now."

"Where are they going?"

"Don't know, but my agents have been busy monitoring the traffic."

"Should we be worried?"

"Probably."

Merl put down the phone. This was the first solid bit of intelligence he had come up with. His soldiering instincts made him tense. He liked to be tense, ready for action. He was never worried, but way in the back of his mind he was getting a little bit concerned. Even the aliens were leaving the planet. This had to be huge. All this trouble because of some damn sissy music.

-35-
THE RED DRAGON

Mount St. Elias is the second largest mountain in North America. It stands 18,008 feet tall. Few have climbed to the summit of the formidable mountain. On reconnaissance flights the team had spotted four possible places where dragons could be, three caves and one large open space several thousand feet up the mountain.

The team set up their base camp on the north side of Mount St. Elias. Dave Kingsley, Newsome Whitmore, and George Marks along with the Geller brothers made several preliminary excursions to scout out trails to the four different goals. Emily went along to film the crew in action.

Barbara Clarence had taken upon herself the role of mom for the expedition and ran the camp kitchen. Rufus spent a lot of time hanging out with Barbara who always had some little tidbit for Rufus to snack on. Paige set herself up in the kitchen area and worked on horoscopes for all the different team members.

Matt Paulson and Mike Kleason spent a while sorting out the various firepower the team had brought along. It had taken dozens of porters on ATVs to bring in all the various guns, ammo, missiles launchers, bows and arrows (arrows dipped in virgin joy tears, of course), steel cables to secure a dragon and more.

Alexander, like all dragons, had keen hearing. He was listening to the sound of many ATV motors far off in the distance. The sound had been going on for several days and was coming from the north side of his mountain. Alexander's cave was high up on the mountain, thousands of feet up. Alexander got up slowly and paced several times around his cave. He was curious about the sounds. He went to the mouth of his cave and looked out at the world. His mountain was, as always, white with snow. The cave itself would have been frozen over if Alexander didn't keep the mouth of the cave open with occasional bursts of flame.

It only took a couple flaps from Alexander's huge wings for him to become airborne. Alexander flew swiftly down the long slopes of Mount St. Elias. About a dozen dragons joined him in the air. The other dragons had heard the thunderous sound of Alexander's wings flapping and had come out to see what was up.

Far down below, the dragons had been spotted by various team members, and the dragons were flying in their direction. It sounded like thunder pouring down from the mountain. Everyone jumped off their ATVs and took cover under the trees. Down at camp Matt Paulson grabbed a bow and a quiver of arrows. He hoped to get at least one or two good shots. Mike Kleason grabbed a shoulder mounted missile launcher.

"You ever use one of those?" asked Matt.

"Nope." replied Mike.

"It has quite a kick, brace yourself."

"Got it."

Matt quickly showed Mike how to load the missile launcher. The thunder of dragons was getting close. Several of the dragons flew rapidly over the trees covering Matt and Mike. Matt waited for a large red dragon that was circling to fly back overhead. He notched an arrow in the bow and tracked the dragon across the sky. After a couple of seconds he let the arrow fly. The arrow struck the dragon under his wing and it let out a hideous cry. The dragon immediately landed on the ground and started uprooting trees looking for the source of the arrow.

Matt and Mike took off running across the forest as quietly as they could. The dragon heard the noise and took off after them. Matt and Mike stopped behind a couple stands of trees and prepared to attack the dragon. Mike loaded a missile into the shoulder launcher, aimed, fired and completely missed. A burst of flame from the dragon roasted Mike and the shoulder launcher.

Matt was a dozen feet away from Mike and the flame just missed him. He felt the withering heat from the blast. Matt notched another arrow in the bow, took aim and let the arrow fly. This time the arrow found its mark and penetrated the left eye of the dragon, going straight to the brain. Apparently there was something to the virgin joy tears. The dragon collapsed on the forest floor.

After the red dragon went down, all hell broke loose. The remaining dragons scattered the base camp and a half dozen of the porters were fried by the thunder of dragons. Paige, Rufus and Barbara had escaped the dragons and were hiding deep in the forest. Stacy Barnett had been asleep in her tent when the dragons descended upon the camp. Her tent was roasted by one dragon's breath. She died in her sleep.

Soon a quiet settled on the forest as most of the dragons returned to their caves. Newsome and the scouting crew returned to the devastated camp several hours later. They had abandoned their ATVs so they wouldn't attract the attention of the dragons, several of which were still flying around the mountain.

Newsome was devastated when they found Stacy's tent, now a smoldering piece of nylon that encased her dead body. It wasn't a pleasant scene. After a while Barbara, Paige and Rufus made their way back to the remains of the base camp. The team was demoralized. It was decided that as soon as Mike and Matt were located the team would retreat for the time being.

Matt wandered into camp several hours later. He was in a state of shock, in spite of his military training, after the death of Mike and the killing of the red dragon. Hours later, after several false starts, Matt led the team to the fallen dragon. The red dragon was over twenty feet in length and had a long pair of horns. The wingspan of the magnificent beast was over forty feet. Newsome made arrangements for the carcass of the dragon to be removed back to Juneau. *Expedition: Dragon Hunt* returned from the back country with tales to tell and the first body of a dragon the world had ever seen.

Once back in Juneau the media descended on the team, along with numerous government agencies claiming jurisdiction over the remains of the dragon. Newsome fought the government fiercely to keep his dragon. Unfortunately, the Department of Interior was finally able to claim the body. Teams of scientists working for the government were eager to get their hands on the body of the dragon to see what they could find out about these strange new beasts.

-36-

BACK HOME, FOR NOW

Half a universe away Jonas was still on the hunt for Trout Gold in the forest on PuloPulo. It had been a leisurely search. Jonas knew they would find the gold eventually and wasn't really worried about how long it was taking. Food and water were plentiful on PuloPulo and there weren't any predators to worry about. As a matter of fact there wasn't another living soul within miles of Jonas and Nathan.

Nathan's sense of smell had led the pair to a small river at the foot of one of the mountains to the northeast of the forest. Nathan was rooting around in the river, carefully pulling nuggets of gold out of the cold water and placing them on the shore. The nuggets were soft, pliable Trout Gold. Jonas filled his backpack with about twenty pounds of the rare yellow metal.

After Jonas had gathered as much Trout Gold as he needed, he called out to Nathan. Nathan flew over and landed next to Jonas. Jonas reached out and touched the top of Nathan's head and the pair disappeared.

In the blink of an eye Jonas and Nathan were back in the San Bernardino Mountains, walking up the path to Jonas' cabin. Jonas

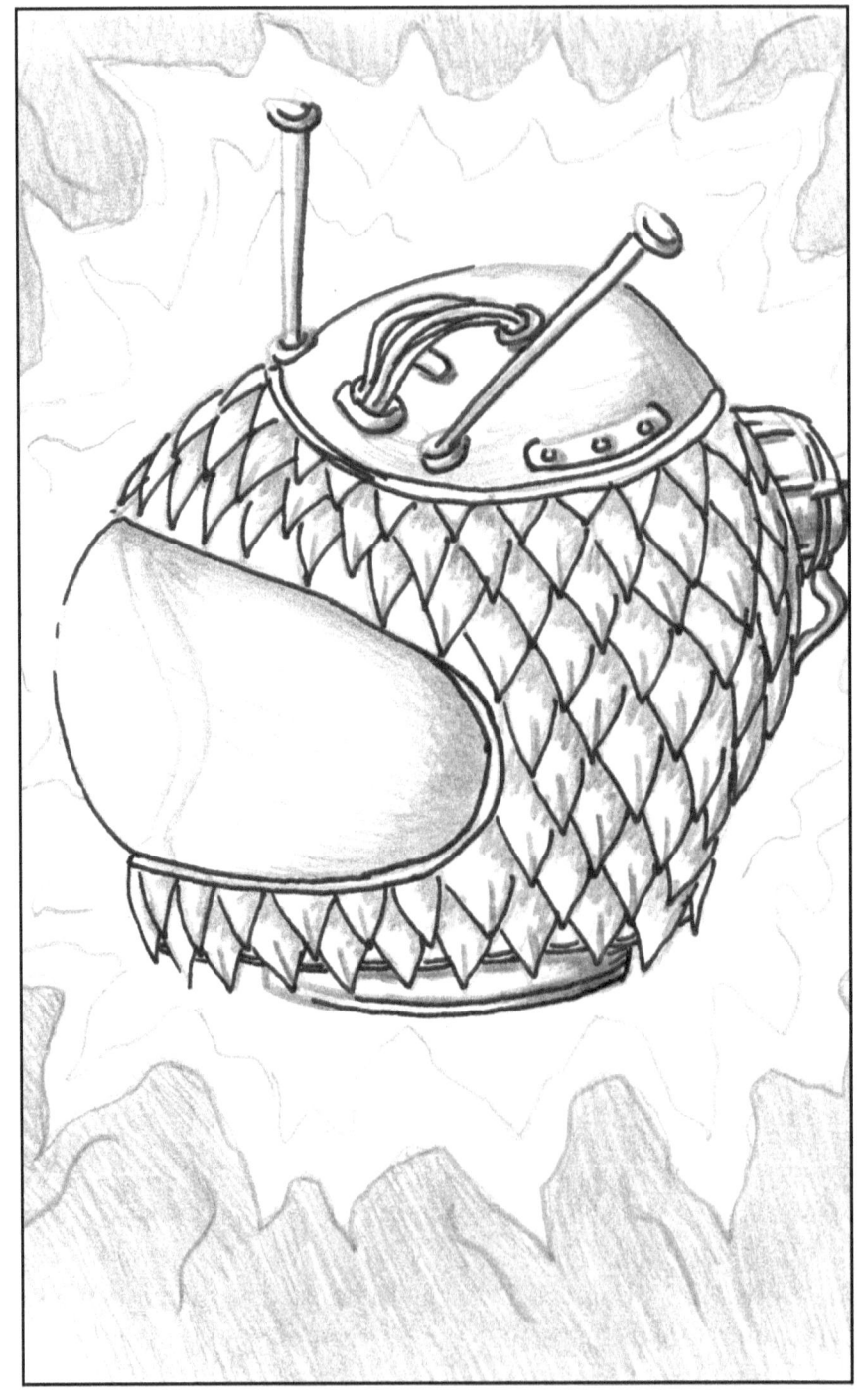

set the backpack full of Trout Gold down on the workbench in his garage, then he and Nathan went into his cabin to make some lunch.

Several days later Celeste came by to check on the cabin and was surprised to find Jonas sitting on the front porch smoking a joint of JK Special.

"Welcome home," said Celeste as she saw her brother.

"Glad to be back," replied Jonas as he handed the joint to Celeste.

"Where did you go this time?"

"Across the Universe, to a planet named PuloPulo."

"Really?" Celeste was, as usual, a bit skeptical of Jonas' claims.

"I wouldn't lie about such a thing."

"What did you go to PuloPulo for?" Celeste took a hit and handed the joint back to Jonas.

"Trout Gold."

"Nice. Did you bring me back any Trout Gold?"

Jonas tossed Celeste a nugget of gold he had been molding into the shape of a small statuette of Nathan the dragon.

"Trout Gold?" said Celeste holding up the small statuette.

"Yup." answered Jonas.

"Sweet," and she tossed the statuette back. The statuette weighed nearly a pound. It was all the gold left over after Jonas had constructed his mind shield. The mind shield was a helmet made of layers of gold like scales, and it did wonders with blocking out psychic noise.

You might be amazed at the amount of psychic noise that is generated by society on a normal day. The greater the density of humanity, the greater the noise. Most people don't ever notice this background noise because they've been hearing it their whole lives.

The mind shield blocked out all this background psychic noise, plus it blocked out the song of Malthusius. There were elaborate electronics involved, and a stainless steel armature. The whole device weighed over twenty-two pounds and was working exactly as the Akashic Records had described. The mind shield created a zone of mental quiet for the wearer, and it had the ability for the wearer to project his thoughts out into the world. Jonah hadn't tried out these abilities yet.

-37-
LOCATION 36°06'38"N
140°05'15"W

Hugo Branson was in love with the world. He had spent so much of his life filled with hate, and thanks to the miracle song in his head he was free from his old life of anger and strife. Now, life was good. He was taking in the fresh air on deck the *Sea Spray III*, one of the vessels in the small fleet of ships that had headed out of the Port of Los Angeles several days earlier. They were headed to a place nearly a thousand miles west of San Francisco to begin their trial cleanup mission.

There were seven ships in the fleet. Several of the boats would be used to haul the trash skimmer, there was a ship that would act as a giant trash compactor, several other ships carried the crew and supplies, and there was a ship for *National Geographic* and various media. Bud Henry had contracted with a Chinese firm to have a giant trash hauling ship rendezvous with them at the clean-up location. The plan was to be out at sea for at least a week.

The weather was crisp and clear in the Pacific Ocean. Cyclone season was around the corner and Bud wanted to get this test done before any storms blew up.

Hugo was leaning over the rail at the front of the ship, watching the bow of the ship cut through the water. The fleet had been traveling at a steady 30 knots for hours. Hugo had been pondering how large the world was, it seemed so big when he was out on the water. The water went on forever in every direction, including down. Hugo had never enjoyed traveling across the ocean before, now he was loving every moment of it. He felt like one happy little particle afloat in the vast universe.

Bud was on the bridge looking over maps for the project. He had lots of maps spread out all over the place with lines, grids and numbers written on them. They were nearing the inner edge of the Great Pacific Garbage Patch. You couldn't see much of the trash on the outer edge, as it floated below the surface, but soon the trash would be visible. For this test Bud was going after the visible trash.

Mike Henry was piloting one of the boats that was modified to be used as a trash skimmer. He couldn't think of anything better to be doing on a Tuesday afternoon then cruising across the ocean at a nice 30 knots. The waves weren't high and the boat cut easily through the water. The boat was called the *Float'em* and was forty-five feet long. It had been owned by Bud's company for seven years and was a solid workhorse. Mike had spent seven years of his young life aboard the *Float'em* and had spent countless hours piloting the boat.

Mike was a happy-go-lucky kind of guy and rarely worried about anything. When people talked about "living in the moment," the phrase was lost on Mike because he always lived in the moment and thought most people did too. He had a girlfriend named Marcia. He thought about Marcia from time to time as he cruised across the open water and the thoughts brought a smile to his face. He snapped a selfie of himself piloting the boat and sent the photo as a text message to Marcia. He included the message: I ♥ U!

The fleet met up with the Chinese trash hauling ship at the appointed location on Wednesday afternoon. The clean-up test was to be conducted Thursday through Saturday. The ocean was soupy with a muck of plastic, chemical sludge, cigarette butts and waste of all kinds. Bud hoped the crew would be able to collect at least fifty tons of garbage, and looking around Bud knew that amount wouldn't even dent the massive garbage pile. The scale of the job ahead was enormous. Of course, you have to start somewhere.

-38-
AFTER THE HUNT

Newsome Whitmore was in a severe funk. He was mourning the death of Stacy Barnett as well as the death of expedition member Mike Kleason. Matt Paulson had related how Mike had died fighting the dragon. Mike had been given a funeral befitting a hero, and his family sprinkled his ashes out at sea off the Monterey Peninsula, Mike's favorite place to dive. Newsome spared no expense for Mike's funeral. George Marks felt personally responsible for Mike's death, and was planning on writing a book about the expedition dedicated to Mike Kleason.

The team had returned to Colorado Springs and was in the process of disbanding. Newsome said they would gather together again, once he had sorted out what had happened, and figured out how to proceed safely in the future.

Paige was glad to see Bessie again. She had left Bessie in the parking lot of the office building of KnewSomeMore Ltd. Paige had earned a nice $40,000 as psychic for the expedition and she planed to invest a little in getting Bessie a thorough tune-up, new tires, new brakes and then take a relaxing drive back to the hi-desert.

Paige and Emily had become good friends on the expedition and Emily planned on visiting Paige the next fall in Joshua Tree. Emily hadn't been out to Joshua Tree in years and once Paige started talking about it she missed it immediately. Until the fall she was going to be working on her next documentary about the dragon expedition.

Dave Kingsley was done with dragons. His executive producer was excited about doing a new series, *DRAGONS: Catch and Release*. Dave said no thanks. Dave wanted a nice, quiet vacation in the Bahamas with a half dozen naked chicks, to further prove his heterosexuality. He invited Matt Paulson to take a vacation with him instead, to unwind. Matt said sure, the Bahamas sounded great after hunting dragons. Matt was enjoying a bit of notoriety as the only person who had ever killed a dragon. Several Hollywood studios were interested in his story.

The expedition had been a big monetary booster for Barbara Clarence. She was not only the famous author of a popular series of dragon books, but now she had actually hunted dragons. Her novels were selling like hotcakes, as they say. The History Channel offered her a new TV series. It was going to be called *Dragons At Large* and would look into the myths and reality of dragons. Barbara said yes.

Molly Pritchard, the virgin, hadn't had her eye operation yet, and was joyfully bottling her tears. She was selling them online. She called her product Molly's Tears and was selling 5oz bottles for $10,000. Matt Paulson endorsed Molly's Tears, for a small fee, and said Molly's Tears were the only virgin joy tears he would use to kill a dragon. Molly was doing really well and had cornered the market on virgin joy tears for dragon hunters.

Newsome, as I mentioned, was in a severe funk. He flew to his vacation home in Martha's Vineyard to collect himself. He had been going out with Stacy Barnett for less than a year and he realized he didn't actually know much about her. As he mourned her death he tried to remember little things about her, like her favorite color. He drew a blank. Stacy's favorite color was red, by the way. It bothered Newsome how little he really missed Stacy and thought he should be feeling worse. Often he would find himself wistfully thinking about Paige Turner instead. He missed her pleasant face and delightful voice. He missed her gypsy ways and her mystic qualities. He missed her dog, Rufus.

-39-
GAME SEVEN

JP stared out through his goalie mask as he watched the play develop. The Kings had slowly brought the puck up the ice and dumped it into the corner. Lang and a Kings' player collided in the corner racing after the puck. The puck squirted free and into the crease. JP dove for the puck and just missed it as a Kings forward flipped the puck over his outstretched glove hand. JP heard the puck ring off the goal post and it bounced in front of his glove. He smothered the puck, the referee blew his whistle and the crowd started cheering madly. *Sometimes you're just living right,* thought JP.

JP had been in the zone for the last several games. All the bounces seemed to be going his way. The Ducks had lost the first three games of the series to Los Angeles and were trying to do the near impossible task of coming back from a 3-0 deficit in the series by winning four games in a row. But it was happening, the team was brimming with confidence now that they had pushed the series to its seventh game. The seventh game was a home game for the Ducks.

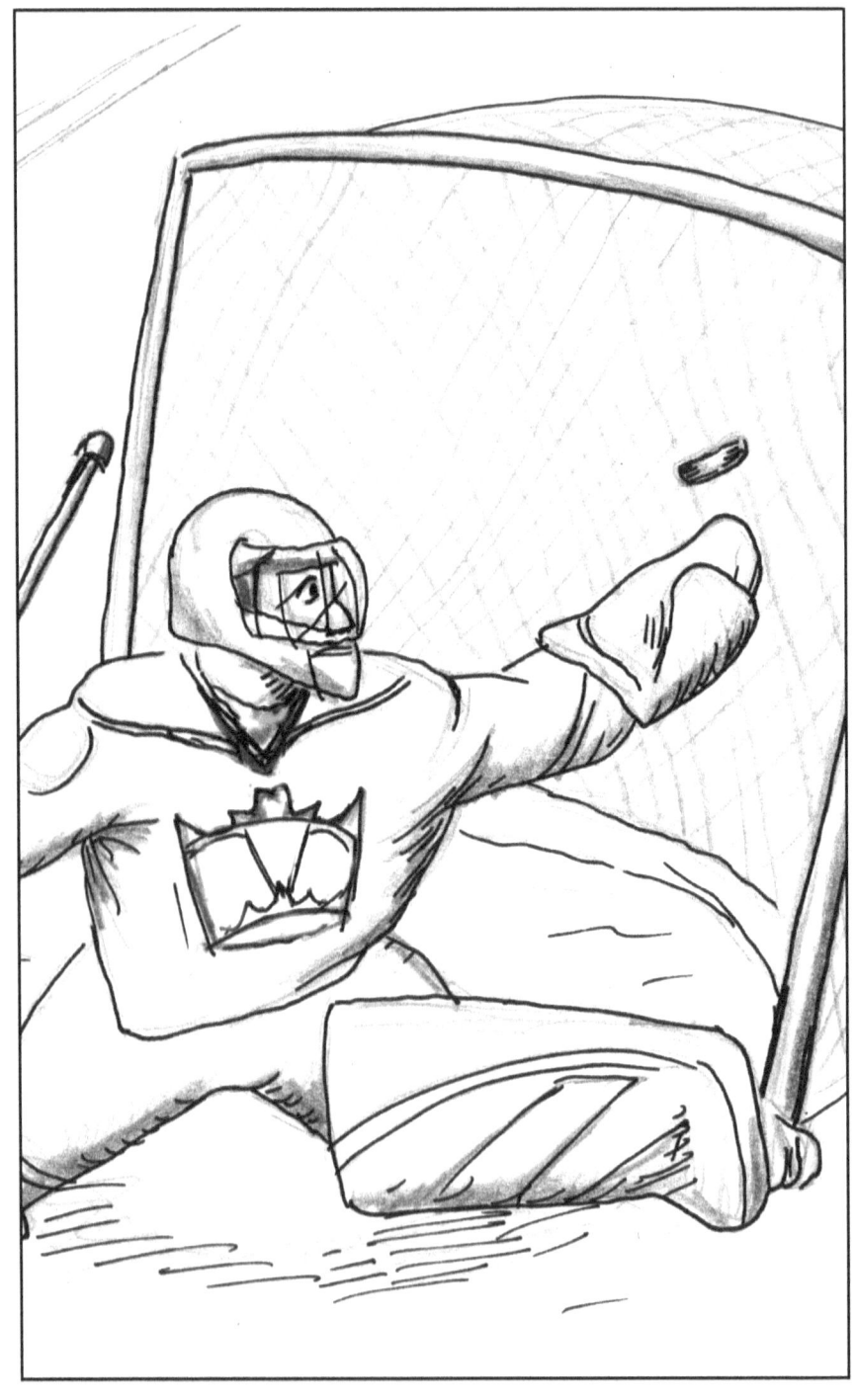

JP glanced up at the clock. There was seven minutes and thirty-eight seconds left in the third period and the score was 1-1. The Ducks were playing their kind of game now. The pace had been hard and fast for the last ten minutes, ever since Lang had scored his twelfth goal of the playoffs three minutes into the third period.

With a few minutes left in the third period the Kings took a penalty for holding and the Ducks went on the power play. The Ducks attacked with everything they had but Mats Daniels was like a brick wall. The clock, in regulation time, ticked down. Three, two, one. The buzzer went off. This game was going into overtime.

The teams retired to their locker rooms for fifteen minutes. A big number five was written on the pad of paper on the wall. The big number five was on everyone's mind. The next team to score was going to the Stanley Cup finals and the other team was going home for the summer.

The Ducks came out with a focused intensity in the first over-time period. The level of play was fast and what you would call, "playoff hockey". This was the reason boys grew up to become hockey players, to play in overtime in a game seven of the Stanley Cup playoffs. Every player on the team stepped up their game. Of course, the Kings did the same thing.

A glorious, picture-perfect moment came when Lang received a big outlet pass and skated in all alone on Mats Daniels. Lang skated straight in and flipped the puck into the top corner of the net. The shot beat Mats' glove hand by a fraction of an inch. The huge video monitors overhead replayed the shot in slow motion as the arena went crazy with cheers and clapping. The monitors started flashing the words "Western Conference Champions". This was the second year in a row the Ducks has won the Conference Championship.

The Ducks' victory had earned them the Clarence S. Campbell

Bowl. The bowl was presented after the teams lined up at center ice to shake hands. The president of the NHL presented the trophy to the Ducks. Lang skated out to receive the Campbell Bowl, but he didn't touch it or lift it. It's considered bad luck in hockey to touch the conference championship trophy. It's like saying you'll settle for this trophy instead of the real trophy, the big prize. For these hockey players, the celebrating wasn't going to happen until they could lift Lord Stanley's Cup, still four victories away.

JP met with the press, showered, put on his street clothes and headed out into the night air. The Southern California June night was perfectly warm. JP took his time driving home to Yorba Linda. He stopped at a Denny's for a post-game meal. No one recognized JP as he ate a Grand Slam breakfast. He checked his social media news feed on his phone while he ate. A bunch of his friends had sent him messages congratulating him on the victory. He responded to a few and sent back thank you messages. He listened to the song of Malthusius in his head. He was used to it now.

Once JP got home he called his brother. Remy had been at the game, thanks to a pair of tickets JP had given him. Remy had taken a date, one of his previous students. The game had been great, the date, not so good.

"Remy, tell me a story," JP said after a few minutes of talking about the game. Remy told JP about Paige and *Expedition: Dragon Hunt*. He had just read an article online in *Rolling Stone* magazine about the tragic ending of the attempt to capture a dragon. JP fell asleep while listening to Remy talk.

-40-
A BETTER WORLD

The songs of Malthusius had become the background sound of the world. The songs had penetrated the collective consciousness in such a subtle way. There were pockets of Malthusius worshipers around the world, or you could say that there were many branches to the Church of Malthusius. About forty percent of the population had been reached by the songs and it continued to deeply effected society in many pleasant ways.

Crisis centers, domestic abuse shelters and suicide hot-lines were all experiencing a drop off in service requests. Hospitals had been emptying out as people were being less effected by psychosomatic and mental illnesses. The United States announced that they were ending their wars overseas and were bringing many of their soldiers home. People had contributed over six million dollars to Bud's ocean cleanup project. The earth was, in general, becoming a better place to live as humans around the planet started to take an interest in cleaning up the world around them.

Major General Merl Dawson was carefully tracking the changes going on in the world. Actually, he had his specialized team working on collecting the data and writing reports which he read with much interest, and disgust. *Damn sissy music was undermining the moral fiber of the whole damn world*, he thought while reading the latest report about marriage and divorce rates. The number of divorces among enlisted men had dropped severely in the last month. Just another sign that things were changing and changing fast.

Just the other night Merl had almost relaxed while watching TV, but luckily he caught himself before he fully relaxed, now he was being extra vigilant. He wasn't going to let this sissy music get to him. Relaxing was just the beginning of a long slide down a slippery slope.

Alexander was also bothered by the songs of Malthusius. High up in his cave in Mount St. Elias he had called a council of dragons. About a dozen dragons, all second and third generation, averaging twenty to thirty feet each, gathered and fit rather tightly into Alexander's cave.

First Alexander called all the dragons to order. There was a definite hierarchy to the council of dragons and the most important senior dragons were closest to Alexander while the smaller, younger dragons were pushed to the back of the cave. After some jostling everyone settled down and Alexander began the meeting.

"How many of you have been hearing a strange musical sound? It's a sound that's constantly playing inside my head, but I'm not hearing it with my ears."

There were many nods and grunts. It seemed that all the gathered dragons could hear the song. Alexander than went on to explain how he had been able to block the song out of his mind most of the time. He also went on to explain that he didn't trust this sound, something about it deeply bothered him. There was something familiar and ancient about this song, to ignore it would be a mistake.

The rest of the dragons agreed with Alexander. Alexander wanted to know who would join him to search for the source of the sound. Because they were a bunch of young dragons, the whole council agreed to join him, adventuring sounded great to them. Older dragons, as you probably know, just like to lay around their caves, usually resting on a big pile of gold.

The next morning the thunder of dragons flew off towards the ocean. Several cruise ships near the glaciers, and thousands of passengers on the ships, heard and saw the thunder of dragons as they passed overhead. The United States Air Force scrambled several jets to monitor, but not engage, the dragons. Two of the dragons from the thunder drove off the fighter jets with flame bursts. The dragons could almost out fly the jets and they nearly toasted one of the fighters before the jets were able to escape.

Alexander led the thunder way out into the Pacific, following the song like a hunter after his prey. He was completely focused on the sound and could feel the song getting stronger and stronger until it had grown extremely intense and rang inside his head. At one point, after several hours of flying, he dove towards the surface and the thunder of dragons followed him deep into the water. They were directly over the castle of Malthusius.

Malthusius could sense the dragons coming. He hadn't had a meal of dragon meat in a millions of years and he was looking forward to dinner.

-41-
DINNER

Malthusius wasn't worried about the dragons. He had dealt with dragons millions of years earlier and they were no threat to him. His mental powers had always won out in the past. Dragons were, after all, only dragons, as far as Malthusius was concerned.

He could almost taste the dragons as they got close to his great house. He could see the whole ocean in his mind and he mentally called dozens of Kraken around the castle. The Kraken could not resist the call of Malthusius and were like puppets under his control. A squad of Kraken left the castle and swam upward to meet the dragons.

Alexander and the thunder of dragons met the Kraken a hundred feet under the surface. The next fifteen minutes roiled the ocean in a chaotic writhing mass of dragon bodies, Kraken tentacles, fire and steam. Alexander found himself wrapped in the tentacles of several Kraken, each one over fifty feet long. He bit and tore at the tentacles but they wouldn't let go and the Kraken were dragging him deeper into the blackness below. From his left a large red dragon appeared and blasted Alexander and the Kraken with flames. Alexander was unscathed by the flames and boiling water but the Kraken lost their grip and Alexander slipped away. Alexander turned in the water and tore after the Kraken that had just had him in their grasp, blasting them with white hot flame, instantly boiling them in the water. Alexander grabbed one of the boiled Kraken and headed towards the surface. *Dinner,* he thought.

Four of the dragons didn't survive the battle and were dragged down into the depths to be eaten by Malthusius. As I mentioned, Malthusius loved the taste of dragon meat.

The remaining members of the thunder of dragons flew slowly black home. Every dragon had pieces of Kraken in their talons. There would be a sad feast of boiled and roasted Kraken that night, high up on Mount St. Elias, as they mourned their lost companions.

Emily Lafleur was watching footage she had taken on the expedition to Mount St. Elias. She had filmed the dragons as they raced down the side of the mountain to attack the base camp below. She hadn't been near enough the camp to film the actual attack, but the footage of the dragons as they flew down the mountain was stunning, especially in slow motion. There was a majesty to the dragons, like they were the royalty of beasts. Emily watched the footage several times and then spliced it into the video she was building.

The documentary was coming together in fits and starts. Emily was surprised that the expedition and the dragon attack had really effected her, now she was having trouble sleeping because she had dragon dreams, scary dragon dreams. Watching the footage and working on the documentary triggered episodes of terror and anxiety. Emily often had to stop and walk away from the project for days at a time.

Meanwhile the Discovery Channel kept calling and wanted to know if the film would be ready for *Dragon Week* in September.

Emily felt like she was going to be crushed by the pressure, so she called Paige to see if she could visit her in Joshua Tree, for a short vacation.

-42-
VISITING JOSHUA TREE

Paige was glad to hear from Emily. She was back at Remy's house in Joshua Tree. She didn't feel like she could invite Emily to stay at Remy's, so she decided to rent a vacation house for a week just outside the entrance to the National Park.

Paige picked up Emily at LAX on a Thursday evening and drove her out to Joshua Tree. The trip took a few hours and the two caught up with each other as Paige drove Bessie on the journey to the hi-desert. Emily told Paige all about the problems she'd been having since the expedition and her anxieties about dragons. Paige told Emily about a healing ceremony she could perform to eliminate the PTSD. It hadn't occurred to Emily that what she was experiencing was PTSD, but it made perfect sense once Paige explained it.

Soon after the two arrived in the hi-desert Emily unpacked, changed her clothes and refreshed her makeup. The two settled on the sofa in the living room of the vacation home. Paige had rolled a joint of some pot she got from her dealer. Her dealer called it JK Special and it was pretty expensive. Her dealer had claimed that it was grown by a cosmic wizard who lived remotely in the San

Bernardino Mountains. Paige assumed her dealer was exaggerating to increase the price.

The joint was, as they say, exquisite. Both Paige and Emily got really stoned but in a most pleasant fashion. Totally relaxed, they watched Emily's incomplete documentary on her laptop. The visuals were amazing, especially as stoned as they were. Later they raided the refrigerator to satisfy their intense cravings for munchies. Rufus followed them around hoping for a handout. Emily fed him some of the french fries they had cooked up. They were having such a good time they didn't bother to turn on the TV and they missed the late night news. Dragons had been sighted in the Lake Tahoe area.

The next day the news was all about dragons again. Paige and Emily caught up with the stories on their social media news feeds in the morning. Dragons in Lake Tahoe! There were a number of posts, but they all showed the same photo of a dragon flying out of the lake. The dragon happened to be Abraham, and he was only twelve feet long. The first generation of dragons hadn't grown as large as the second and third generations. In the photo Abraham had a large rainbow trout in his mouth. The photo was taken by a retired electrician who was out fishing on the lake when he had spotted the dragon swimming under water. He had gotten out his camera just in time to capture the spectacular photo of Abraham bursting out of the water. The photo had gone viral.

Emily and Paige discussed driving to Lake Tahoe but decided against it. "Enough dragons for now," is how Emily had put it. She wanted to hike around, scramble on boulders, chase lizards – small lizards, and relax, especially relax. On the second night they went down to the Joshua Tree Saloon for dinner. The place was packed but they found a couple stools at the bar. Cassie Stackwell was tending bar that night and came over to say hi to her old friend, Paige. Paige introduced Cassie to Emily. The three exchanged small talk over the next few hours while Paige and Emily ate dinner.

Cassie, as it turned out, was a fan of Emily's documentaries. She had seen both of her "famous" documentaries on the Independent Film Channel: *The Raft* about a group of penguins, and *If I Were A Duck* about the life of a mallard duck. Emily blushed when Cassie went on about how much she loved her documentaries and especially Little Jojo, the penguin star of *The Raft*. Everyone loved Little Jojo. The two left the saloon before the evening's entertainment began, and they missed out on hearing the remarkable guitar and harmonica blues duo, Hank and Henry.

On Sunday Remy drove out from Long Beach and visited with Paige and Emily. Paige had still been taking the micro-doses of magic mushrooms Remy had prescribed, but her supply was getting low. Remy brought several pounds of mushrooms with him when he visited, and the three ended up spending Sunday evening baking pretty hard.

They all put on headlamps and explored the desert at night. It was magical. They looked for flying saucers but none arrived. Instead, the green mushroom elf showed up with some words of wisdom for Emily about her PTSD. Later, as the mushrooms were wearing off Paige rolled up a joint of JK Special. Remy was familiar with JK Special, he called it Wizard Weed. He said Wizard Weed was grown by some mystic wizard who lived in the San Bernardino Mountains. He knew the wizard's sister, Celeste.

It was that magical time of three in the morning when they gathered on the porch to smoke the joint. It was a pleasant eighty-two degrees. Paige lit the joint, took a big hit and held it in. She passed the joint over to Emily who did the same. The joint passed to Remy and he cupped the joint in his hands and took a deep hit. A smooth and euphoric feeling enveloped the group as they continued to pass the joint around. There was something truly special about JK Special.

For some reason Remy started talking about his younger brother, JP, and the Stanley Cup playoffs. Emily, as it turned out, was a big hockey fan. She was familiar with Jean-Paul Lafleur, the outstanding goaltender for the Anaheim Ducks. She was pleasantly surprised to find out JP was Remy's brother, and she peppered him with questions. After a bit of conversation Remy and Emily realized they were distantly related. Remy started calling Emily "little sister". Emily had always wanted to make a hockey documentary and now the gears in her brain were starting to turn. *How about a documentary about a hockey goalie,* she thought.

-43-

WAITING FOR THE PUCK TO DROP

Hockey is not the most popular sport in the United States, not even the second or third most popular. Meanwhile, it's the national sport of Canada. This is generally attributed to the climates of the two different countries. Canada is universally cold and icy during the winter, while the climate varies wildly across the United States. The warmer the area, the less interest in ice hockey it seems.

Whatever the reason, in Southern California, hockey was barely on the radar for most people. Even well-known hockey players like Lang Nichols could go about their daily business without being recognized, something that would never happen in a place like Montreal. Not one of JP's neighbors in Yorba Linda had any idea that a world-class goaltender lived on their street, unlike on the east coast.

Tony Lacroix couldn't go anywhere in Pittsburgh without people recognizing him. The Pittsburgh Penguins had defeated the New York Rangers and won the Eastern Conference Championship. They were awarded the Prince of Wales Trophy for their efforts. Their captain, Tony Lacroix, picked up the trophy and skated it around the ice, in defiance of the old superstitions. *One trophy down, one to go*, thought Lacroix as he skated the trophy off the ice and headed towards the locker room.

The Stanley Cup, the National Hockey League's premier trophy, is the oldest and most revered prize in modern sports. None of the history, or the excitement of the moment was lost on JP. He could hardly believe that he was going to play for the Cup. He had called Remy, just to talk about the moment, but Remy was visiting friends in Joshua Tree. Remy invited JP to join them, but JP was too busy with getting ready for the last series of the season, the most important games of the whole year. It was decided that after the series they'd get together. The two were always making plans for JP to come visit, later.

The Stanley Cup finals were going to begin the upcoming Monday in Anaheim. Getting ready for the next round of the play-offs included a few sessions with the goaltending coach. The coach was always trying to get JP back to the fundamentals of the game and all his drills dealt with the little details of JP's playing. After a few games JP would fall back on old habits, get a little fancy in his play, and not pay strict attention to the basics. That's when JP would give up bad goals. Then the coach would run him through some special drills during practice. Over the second half of the season JP became a much better player, and now it was paying off.

The head coach was keeping the press away from JP. He didn't want his starting goaltender losing his focus. When JP wasn't at practice on Saturday and Sunday he was at home watching game videos the training staff prepared for him. But mostly JP waited for Monday night, for the puck to drop. He wanted to get on with the game. All he could do was wait.

-44-
THE ART OF ROMANCE

Paul LePaul flew up to visit Der in Eugene several weeks before the art opening. Paul stood out like a sore thumb in Eugene, but then again, so did Der. He reveled in being Eugene's most flamboyant character. Nobody wore such colorful outfits with as much style and panache as Der. He wined and dined Paul like a proper lady, which made Paul feel really special. Der and Paul were passionate about their relationship.

Der had been thinking about his relationship with Paul a lot before Paul had flown up for a visit. The two had been dating for only eight months, but Der had never felt the way he did about Paul with anyone before. He was sure it was love. He had bought a diamond ring and was going to propose to Paul on the night of the opening. He told Dela about his plans to surprise Paul with a ring.

"I'm going to go down on bended knee and everything," Der told Dela. They were busy looking over the layout for the catalog for the show. The catalog layouts had to get to the printer the next day to be ready in time.

"So you want to propose in the gallery, not at an intimate dinner?" Dela imagined how nice the scene of a proposal during an intimate dinner looked in her head. She made a note to take her girlfriend out somewhere special soon.

"Nope, I like to call it the art of romance. I have to propose in an art gallery. Plus, all our friends should be there that night. I want the proposal to make a big splash."

"So, where are you planning to marry this lucky man?"

"I was thinking about Joshua Tree... in California."

"Joshua Tree? Why?"

"There is a place out there called Hicksville Trailer Palace. Very kitschy with a bunch of unique trailers and a pool. We can rent the whole place and have a big party. It's 420 friendly."

"420 friendly?"

"You can smoke pot everywhere. It's awesome."

Der showed Dela the website on her computer.

"Nice," said Dela, "I hope I'm invited to the wedding."

"I was hoping you'd be my best man, or best person."

"I'd be honored," replied Dela, surprised that Der had asked her.

Later the conversation turned to the song of Malthusius and the recent sighting of a dragon in Lake Tahoe. The dragons were always in the news lately.

"We live in strange times" said Der, stating the obvious.

-45-
AN ANCIENT WAR

Malthusius had a new song to sing. This one was a powerful song, a song to capture the whole world. The humans had proven to be susceptible to his mind control and large portions of the population were effectively under a kind of hypnosis. This new song would take care of the rest of the population and hopefully the pesky dragons.

People often wonder what killed off the dinosaurs millions of years ago, it was Malthusius. He hunted them down one by one and eliminated the whole civilization. The dragons, or dinosaurs, had once almost killed Malthusius, but Malthusius had won that war sixty-four million years ago.

The war had come when the dragons had existed for ages and were at the height of their civilization. Millions of dragons of various shapes, sizes and species lived all around the world. They would gather together in great councils. They were much more intelligent than humans are today.

Malthusius had been Lord of the Earth for as long as any dragon could remember. Even though the dragons could block out the calling songs of Malthusius, they recognized that he was a much greater power. But he would go away for long periods of time, and he didn't effect the dragons too much. For a million years an uneasy truce existed between the dragons and Malthusius.

What had changed things was that Malthusius started to eat the dragons. He had sent out a powerful song one day and a dozen young dragons had responded to his call, unable to resist like the older dragons could. It was a massacre as Malthusius devoured the whole group.

A council of older dragons was called and it was decided that Malthusius had to go. It was time for the dragons to rule the planet. The dragons launched attack after attack against Malthusius. But Malthusius resisted all the attacks and killed many of the dragons using a vast puppet army of Kraken. The Kraken numbered in the tens of thousands in those days. After the numerous dragon attacks against Malthusius, he retaliated, fiercely, with no mercy.

No dragon had been able to resist the single, focused mental energies that Malthusius possessed. He literally blew dragons apart with his mind. They could not hide from Malthusius as he tracked down every last dragon in the world. The battles continued for years. Malthusius eventually won.

Malthusius had been wounded many times during the war with the dragons, and was battle scarred. He had lost several tentacles, but they grew back over time. He had slept for thousands of years after he destroyed the dragons, and as he slept he dreamed of a new world, and a new world began to grow upon the face of the Earth and the kingdom of mammals arose.

Visiting alien species came and went from the planet. Eventually, after millions of years passed, and Malthusius had slept and woken numerous times, a group of humanoid aliens from a planet circling a dying sun in the Andromeda Galaxy found the planet uninhabited and settled down. They called the planet Earth. Then Malthusius went to sleep again for fifteen thousand years.

The humanoids flourished on the planet, and soon many, many generations of humanoids had lived and died on Earth. The people forgot they had come from somewhere else and they imagined that they had always lived on the Earth. They invented stories and gods to explain their creation.

Now Malthusius had awakened to find these humans had grown to over seven billion individuals covering the planet and they had made a disaster of his home. Malthusius considered the humans to be a form of vermin (tasty vermin, but vermin all the same) that needed to be exterminated just like he had exterminated the dragons long ago. And that's why he was lulling them with his songs. Soon he would be feeding on a nearly endless supply of tasty human vermin snacks, lining up, ready to throw themselves into his waiting mouth.

And as for these new dragons, he wasn't even concerned.

-46-
LOOKING FOR DRAGONS

A lexander sat in his cave and pondered the situation for several days. Two things were bothering him now and he wasn't sure what to do, but he was going to do something. The first problem was the source of the sound. Now that he had found out where it was coming from, he wasn't sure how to eliminate it. But he had never experienced a fight like that one under the sea, and he was spoiling for another. Like I mentioned before, Alexander loved a good fight.

The other problem concerning him was these humans. They were everywhere, and they seemed threatening. They had killed a close friend of his, one of the red dragons. Smoke slowly trickled out of Alexander's nostrils as he sat pondering these things. Soon he got up, went to the mouth of his cave, and within two beats of his wings had launched into the air.

Alexander flew around the mountain and let out several tremendous cries. He was calling another council of dragons. Within the hour a dozen dragons had gathered in Alexander's cave. He quickly got to the point of the council meeting.

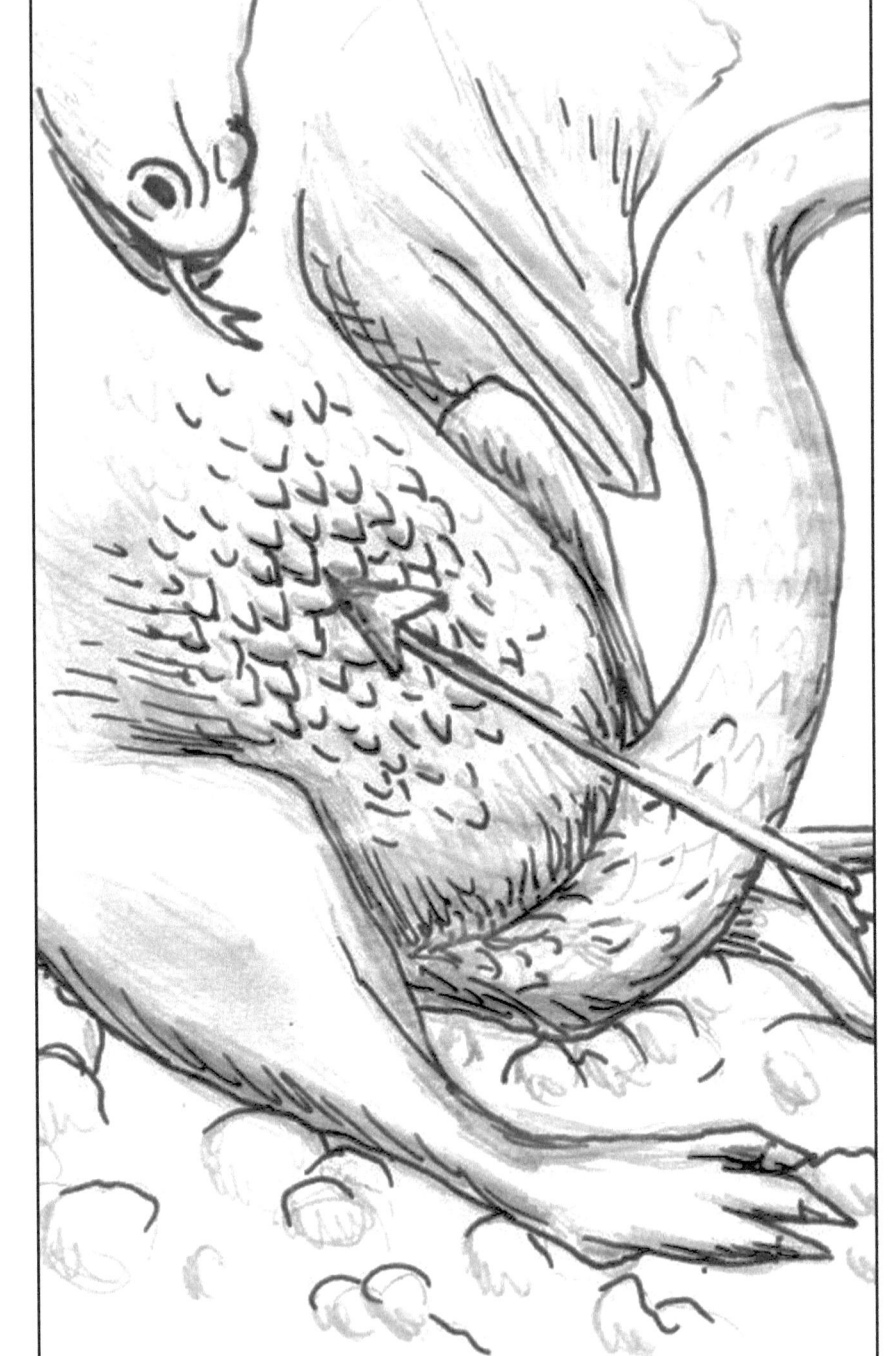

"I am sure there are other dragons like us in the world, and we must gather them together," began Alexander. He laid out his concerns about the humans, and the ongoing problem with the sound.

Alexander knew they needed much greater numbers to deal with both situations. He asked the dragons to fly out into the world and find other dragons and bring them back to the mountain.

"I am going to fly south," announced Alexander, and all the other dragons announced where they were going to go. Without delay the dragons flew off on their missions.

The mission ahead was perilous for all the dragons involved. Dragons are by nature social creatures but only within their own tribes. Between tribes they are territorial. Fortunately, all dragons speak the same language and most dragons will negotiate rather than fight. Alexander, who was a massive dragon, did better when it came to negotiating. The littler dragons didn't do so well.

Malthusius, in his castle deep under the Pacific Ocean, noted the movement of Alexander and the dragons. He was tracking Alexander as he flew south from Alaska and out over the Pacific Ocean towards the west coast of the United States. Alexander was planning on exploring the coastal waters and rivers, all the way down to Antarctica if necessary. Being a dragon he knew exactly where to look for other dragons. The other dragons on his council had flown towards Russia, China and Europe. A trio of dragons had flown towards Africa.

Alexander and his council weren't the only ones looking for dragons. Dragon huntering had become a cottage industry overnight. Armed with cameras, video equipment, guns and arrows dipped in virgin joy tears, these self-professed dragon hunters had descended on Lake Tahoe. Barbara Clarence was there with the film crew of *Dragons At Large*, hoping to capture a dragon on film.

Abraham, one of the original dragons, lived with his lady dragons, Celeste and Edie, in a remote part of the lake. They did their best to avoid humans and for the most part they had been successful. That is, until Abraham had been photographed coming out of the water with a large trout in his mouth. Unfortunately, the little family of dragons didn't realize they were currently an internet sensation, and the focus of a number of humans crazed with the idea of killing a dragon.

It took the dragon hunters a few days to find the lair of Abraham and his ladies. Abraham was the first one shot at by the dragon hunters. Fortunately they were using a shot gun and the buckshot bounced harmlessly off of Abraham's scales. Both Abraham and Celeste made it high into the sky, and out of range in time, but Edie wasn't so lucky. Edie had been struck by an arrow dipped in Molly's Tears and the arrow tore right through her scales like a hot knife through butter. Several more arrows hit her and she tumbled out of the sky and crashed into the lake. She was dead before she hit the water. The film crew of *Dragons At Large* caught the whole thing on video.

The two remaining dragons flew off into the Sierra Mountains where they grieved for several days over the loss of their mate and companion. Then they flew to the ocean to live somewhere off the coast. That is where Alexander found them. They agreed to join Alexander on his quest and the three of them continued south.

-47-
THE FINALS

The Ducks won the first two games of the finals series at home, the Penguins won the next two games in Pittsburgh. All the games had been close, and the games in Pittsburgh had gone into overtime. JP wasn't in the zone, but he was playing outstanding hockey. Most of the bounces seemed to be going his way, and his defensemen were doing a great job of keeping people out of his crease.

Now it was mid-way through the first period of the fifth game and JP couldn't get this crazy, infectious song out of his head. It was distracting him something awful. He stood in his goal crease watching the action up the ice. He rarely paid any attention to the crowd, but tonight he looked around, and it seemed like the whole building was moving to the song in his head. Then the building began to spin as JP felt waves of vertigo wash over him. After a few seconds, he collapsed on the ice.

The referee blew his whistle and the play stopped. The medical staff rushed out on the ice to attend to JP. After a few anxious minutes, JP got to his feet and skated off the ice under his own power. The crowd stood up and gave him a standing ovation. Mark Russell came in to relieve him in goal.

In the locker room the medical staff decided that JP was de-hydrated and started an IV to re-hydrate him. JP laid on his back as the IV dripped into his arm, listening to the song in his head. He watched the game on the TV in the locker room. The Penguins were pounding away at Mark Russell, throwing everything they had at him, trying to score on the relief goaltender before he was warmed up. Mark did a stand up job, and the game was scoreless at the end of the first period.

Mark Russell played the rest of the game, and the Ducks won 3-2. JP was feeling much better when the team boarded a plane three hours later at John Wayne Airport headed to Pittsburgh. The pad of paper on the locker room wall had one piece of paper left on it, on that piece of paper was a big number one.

They say that an elimination game is the hardest game to win in the Stanley Cup. Mark Russell started in goal for the game in Pittsburgh. Mark Russell had been born and raised in Pittsburgh, and had grown up dreaming of playing for the hometown team. Tony Lacroix had once been a hero of Mark's, now he was facing him on the ice. Lacroix beat Russell three times that evening and scored a hat trick. The Penguins won the game 5-3. It was a bitter-sweet night for Mark. The team got back on the plane several hours later, and headed back to Southern California for the last game of the year.

-48-
THE NEW WAR

Malthusius was on the move. His latest song was going to be a hit, he knew it, and he was beginning his victory tour. It was time for the world of humans to meet their Lord and Master.

The house of Malthusius began to rise from the bottom of the ocean once again. An earthquake rocked the Pacific Ocean. The earthquake was merely for effect, caused by Malthusius concentrating his mental powers on an undersea fault line.

The earthquake wasn't felt by Bud Henry and his crew busy cleaning up the Pacific Ocean. The test of the equipment had gone well, and they had stayed out in the Garbage Patch for an extra week doing more cleanup. The skimmer device had collected over two hundred and fifty tons of garbage with a minimum amount of fish. The trash compactor ship had broken down twice trying to keep up with the collection effort.

Now Bud and his crew were winding up operations. Today was going to be the last day of skimming. Hugo Branson stood on deck and surveyed the scene. Malthusius looked out through his eyes. Hugo was now completely under the control of Malthusius, docile as a lamb. He hummed the song of Malthusius. The job he had been given, the vision of cleaning up the ocean, was going well and for that Malthusius filled Hugo with a sense of well-being. Hugo, for all he knew, was overjoyed with this new arrangement.

Many people were happy with the new situation where Malthusius did all their thinking for them. Thousands of people were just as hypnotized as Hugo was, including Wolf Thomas. His Church of Malthusius had maxed out at fifty-two people. He just couldn't let any more people camp on his land, and he had no other alternative but to turn away sincere worshipers of Malthusius. It broke his heart to turn people away. Malthusius couldn't help but feel satisfied while staring out through the eyes of Wolf Thomas, because he could see how effective his song was. These humans were too easy to control. Malthusius felt invincible and it felt good.

Meanwhile, a large thunder of dragons was flying across the waters of the South Pacific. Alexander had been convincing while on his quest, and had collected many recruits to his mission. Two hundred and thirteen dragons were now flying to the end of South America where a large number of dragons lived. Around the world the various missions had been successful, probably because dragons are so smart that they know when to come together for a common cause. All over the world large thunders of dragons were soon flying towards Mount St. Elias in Alaska.

This mass movement of dragons did not go unnoticed by the human population of the planet. Many nations scrambled their various Air Forces to investigate the reports of large numbers of flying dragons. Around the world dozens of jet fighters went down in flames as they tried to attack the thunders of dragons. The news on TV and the internet was about a new war. War between the humans and the dragons. This caused a mass panic around the Earth. To the dragons, these fighter attacks proved that the humans were a big problem that needed to be dealt with sooner or later.

The dragons began descending on Mount St. Elias on June fifteenth, which happened to be the same day as the final game of the Stanley Cup, not that the two events were related. The city of Juneau and the surrounding areas were evacuated in a panic. The Stanley Cup playoffs were the last thing on the mind of any of the residents of Juneau.

Down in Eugene, Der and Paul LePaul were glued to their television, watching the news about the amazing events going on. Experts had suggested that several thousand dragons had already landed on a mountain called St. Elias in Alaska. The news reports were both fascinating and terrifying. Somehow, CNN had gotten an amazing video of hundreds of dragons flying around the top of the mountain. Their bodies cast haunting silhouettes against the white snow of the mountain. It was hard for most people to grasp that what they were watching was really happening on earth and wasn't just a movie. The lead anchor person on CNN called this "the greatest threat mankind has ever faced".

In Juneau, the Geller bothers, Hans and Ulrick, had not evacuated. Not when such a prime opportunity had presented itself. ABC had hired the brothers to get exclusive footage of the dragons from the base of the mountain. Hans and Ulrick were going into the back country armed with cameras, video equipment and arrows dipped in virgin joy tears. The Geller brothers were, as usual, brimming with over-confidence.

Paige and Emily watched the news from the rented vacation home in Joshua Tree. Emily had stayed an extra week, and the two were completely wrapped up in the news from Alaska. It had been just a few weeks since they had been at the mountain and now there weren't only a dozen or so dragons in the world, there were thousands.

Newsome Whitmore watched the news with a deep, obsessive fascination. He chartered a flight to Alaska. He wanted to get as close to the action as possible. While nearly everyone was evacuating Juneau, Newsome slipped in unnoticed. There was equipment from *Expedition: Dragon Hunt* being stored in a warehouse in the city. Newsome got a four-wheel-drive truck, some supplies, a bow, and a quiver of arrows dipped in virgin joy tears. He also grabbed the remaining shoulder missile launcher and a case of custom fire extinguisher shells. He headed out of the city towards Mount St. Elias. What he was going to do, he had no idea, but he guessed that he'd figure it out once he got to the mountain.

Across the United States, all the branches of the military were put on high alert and troops began to mobilize. A war song was pounding in everyone's head. Malthusius was monitoring the human mobilization against the dragons with great satisfaction, and was singing a war song to motivate the humans to fight. *It's good to be king*, thought Malthusius.

Meanwhile, in Boise, the Anti-Cephalopod Front had had enough of the song of Malthusius and choose this moment to strike the Aquarium. Or, attempted to strike the Aquarium. They had pipe bombs, machetes and several guns which they tried to smuggle into the Aquarium, which was having a special exhibition of jelly fish. "A jelly fish isn't a cephalopod, but it's close enough," Jerry had remarked.

The five members of the A.C.F. didn't make it as far as the special exhibition. Security, which had been increased since the recent Aquarium attack, quickly apprehended them just inside the entrance. The A.C.F. members were all dressed the same in black tactical gear, wearing identical backpacks. They had waited patiently together in line to enter the building. They looked menacing in their black, wrap-around sunglasses and when security looked into their backpacks, well, that was the end of their attack. The FBI took charge of the case and now Jerry and his four cohorts had disappeared into the Federal criminal justice system, never to be heard from again, at least not in this book.

-49-
THE GRAND COUNCIL

The dragons created a great clearing at the base of Mount St. Elias. They uprooted many trees and created a great pile of the trunks in the center of the clearing. There was room for hundreds of the great beasts to gather in the clearing and a grand council of dragons began, the first one on Earth in over sixty-four million years.

Alexander landed in the clearing and lit the pile of trees on fire with a white hot burst from his mouth. In dragon society this meant the council had begun. Alexander was clearly the largest dragon in the gathering and the only one whose scales were covered in gold. The fire light glinted off of him. It was an impressive sight.

Alexander addressed the assembled grand council and spoke of his concerns about the sound, the song coming from the Pacific Ocean. Griffin, a large dragon from Scotland spoke up and suggested that the humans were a much more important problem. There was a murmur of agreement among the gathered dragons. A delegation of dragons from Patagonia suggested the whole group fly south to the tip of South America where they had been living free from the presence of humans. A group of dragons from deep in the forests of Russia suggested the same plan for their area. Many of the dragons spoke up that it had been foolish to come out of hiding.

The grand council continued until dawn, several resolutions were passed. Alexander had argued late into the night about why he was deeply bothered by the songs that had troubled his mind. He talked of an intelligence deep in the ocean that was sinister and evil, a presence that would always be a threat to the world of dragons, even more of a threat than the humans. Already four dragons had died fighting the source of the sound, their lives needed to be avenged. Many dragons were swayed by Alexander's persuasive arguments. It was generally agreed that the sound that was troubling them was a priority and a resolution was passed that Alexander and a thousand dragons would go try and solve that problem. Another resolution was passed that the dragons were now at war with the humans.

Alexander and a massive thunder of dragons darkened the sky for several miles as they left for the Pacific the next day. A thousand dragons in a wide variety of colors poured over the edge of the glacier and out to sea. Thousands of passengers were watching from two cruise ships as the dragons approached. The ships were in the process of evacuating the area due to the dragon threat. The thunder passed over the cruise ships and scorched them with their breath. The ships were left in flames. There were no civilians in the war between humans and dragons, and the dragons were ready for a fight.

Malthusius sensed the approach of the massive thunder. His castle now rested on the surface of the water. He waited for the dragons to get nearer. He thought about the fact that he was about to feast on an endless supply of dragon meat. *Yum*, thought Malthusius.

-50-
THE GAME

There are games, and then there is THE GAME. Tonight was going to be THE GAME.

I may be biased, but nothing beats the excitement of game seven in the finals of the Stanley Cup playoffs — nothing. The level of intensity and focus is amazing. The pace is fast, the passing and checking, quick and hard. The sound of the crowd, thunderous. Tonight the Stanley Cup would be awarded to one of the teams on the ice. There was nothing else to prepare for, this was IT.

JP sat crouched in the goal crease, watching the puck in the hand of the referee halfway up the ice. The referee blew his whistle and brought everyone to attention, players put the blades of their sticks on the ice ready for the faceoff. JP glanced up at the clock. Only three periods of twenty minutes each and he could be lifting the Stanley Cup. *Focus*, he told himself.

The puck dropped and Lang won the faceoff and dished the puck off to his right winger. Tony Lacroix knocked Lang down to the ice for his efforts. The game was on. It was going to be a punishing affair. The Penguins set the pace right away. They played the same fast-paced game the Ducks liked to play, but for the first

five minutes it was all Penguins controlling the puck. As the period wore on the Ducks started to find their skating legs. The Penguins took a bad penalty and the Ducks scored on the ensuing power play. Fifty-eight seconds later the Ducks scored again. The noise level inside the arena was deafening.

Between periods the Ducks sat quietly in the locker room. There was nothing to be said that hadn't been said already. Twenty minutes down, forty minutes to go.

The second period was hard fought by both teams, but there was no change in the score.

In the third period the Penguins came out on fire, like men possessed. The intensity of the game increased to a whole new level. It took Pittsburgh only three minutes and twenty-three seconds to score a goal off a deflection in front of the net. It took them another two minutes and twenty-four seconds to score a second goal on multiple rebounds. With the score tied, the teams gathered to faceoff at center ice. It was a fourteen minute, thirteen second game now.

JP tried to push the last two goals out of his mind. The Cup seemed to be getting close to slipping out of his grasp and he pushed that thought out of his mind too. JP skated back and forth creating a little snow in front of his goal. He slapped his stick blade down on the ice. He crouched in his goalie stance. He focused.

The teams battled back and forth for the next ten minutes. The pace was fast and tight. Each team had several grade A opportunities. No one was making any mistakes on the ice now. The crowd was restless with anticipation for what would happen next.

What happened next was a simple pass up ice from Tony Lacroix to his left winger. The winger had the puck bounce off his stick and into the path of an onrushing Duck defenseman. The defenseman made a quick, short pass to Lang who was streaking up the ice. Lang dished the puck off to his right winger who was flying up the ice with him. The winger passed the puck back to Lang who was now at the top of the crease. Lang unloaded a shot just inches off the ice and beat the Pittsburgh goaltender on the five hole, right between the pads. The red goal light went on, and the Honda Center erupted in deafening cheers, applause, etc.

There was still three minutes and forty-three seconds left in the game.

The puck dropped at center ice and Pittsburgh came on like a fury. They weren't going to let the Cup slip from their fingers without a fight. Not until they had left every ounce of energy out there on the ice. JP faced six shots in the next few minutes, several of them grade A opportunities. He stayed square to the shooter, he kept the blade of his stick on the ice, he kept his glove hand to the side of his body, loose and ready. Time slowed down and he entered the zone.

The Penguins pulled their goaltender for an extra attacker with one minute and fifty-two seconds left to go in the game. JP was a wall in front of his goal. He felt as big as a house. The Penguins fired shot after shot but JP stopped them all. The clock ticked down. Three, two, one last shot and a save. The buzzer sounded. The Ducks had won the Stanley Cup!

The team mobbed JP. Sticks and gloves were scattered on the ice. Several members of the training staff skated out on the ice to hand out hats to the team that said Stanley Cup Champions. There were a lot of high fives and fist bumps as the team lined up at center ice to shake hands with their vanquished opponents. Meanwhile preparations were being made to present Lord Stanley's Cup.

The president of the NHL presented the Cup to the team's captain, Lang Nichols. Lang skated around the rink holding the thirty-four pound trophy over his head. The crowd went wild. Lang passed the trophy off to his assistant captain Dougie Blake. Dougie was a twenty year veteran and had almost given up hope he'd ever get to skate the Cup. As he skated around the rink he felt that life was complete, and he thought about retiring. Dougie passed the Cup off to JP. JP held up the Cup and then lowered it down and planted a big kiss on the Cup. The crowded roared its approval. JP skated around the rink. He hoped Remy was watching on TV somewhere.

Remy had been watching the game, first at the Joshua Tree Saloon and later back at home. While at the Saloon, Remy had kept pointing out to whoever would listen that the goaltender on the TV was his brother. Nobody was much interested in what Remy was saying except Cassie. Cassie had met JP several times and was glad to see he was doing well.

Remy had several large sixteen ounce Sculpin IPAs by the time he left for home. He had eaten a meal while drinking, so he was only a little bit tipsy. Here's what Remy had eaten while drinking and watching the hockey game: a dozen jalapeno poppers, a blue cheese burger, well done, with a side of french fries, extra crispy. He ordered a side of mayonnaise to dip the french fries in, and he had a dinner salad. Before he left he ordered a BLT to go. He tipped Cassie over twenty percent when he paid his bill, as usual.

It was well into the third period when Remy got home. He turned on his TV in time to see Lang's game winning goal. He watched the presentation of the Cup, feeling really great for his brother. He felt a special kind of pride as he watched JP skate the Cup around Honda Center.

Later on, the phone woke Remy from his sleep. He had fallen asleep on the sofa watching the post-game show.

"Remy, tell me a story," came JP's voice on the other end of the line. JP sounded a little buzzed, he said there had been a lot of champagne in the locker room that night. Remy told JP about a great hockey game he had watched that evening. The story had a happy ending.

-51-
THE BATTLE

Alexander was tuned into the sound of the song with an intense focus. He led the thunder of dragons far out into the ocean. Malthusius was aware that the dragons were coming and he started to call out to them. He called them to himself. He called them towards their death.

As the thunder of dragons approached Malthusius began focusing on individual dragons. The full mental powers of Malthusius were brought to bear on the various dragons, and they started to explode in mid-air. In spite of this, the dragons continued to fly onward, towards the source that was calling them. Many of the dragons found the call irresistible. As they flew onward dragon after dragon exploded in the air.

Alexander quieted his mind and increased his speed. All around him his companions were exploding. Up ahead he sensed the source of this massacre. He saw a small island and he dove towards it. The remaining thunder of dragons followed him.

Malthusius remained calm, but was getting a little tense. The giant dragon leading the thunder was a problem. He kept trying to focus on him but he couldn't quite narrow his thoughts on it like he could on the other dragons.

Thousands of miles away, Jonas Knight was sitting on the porch of his cabin. He had his mind shield on his head and was concentrating on a mental disturbance going on out in the Pacific. He had started to pick up the thoughts of a dragon, a large dragon, it seemed. The dragon was intensely focused.

Jonas was perplexed by the way the device was working and tried out different settings. It was the first time he had used it at full capacity. The mind shield could pick up and send mental vibrations as well as shielding him from them. And now he was picking up the strong dragon thoughts, garbled and mixed in with the song of Malthusius. He concentrated on the source of the song, the ancient Malthusius, and sent a withering mental blast to try and stop the music. A torrent of mental confusion hit Malthusius, and stunned him for a moment. That was unexpected. He had never experienced anything like it.

All around Alexander his companions suddenly stopped exploding. The thunder pressed on, diving down towards the island with its giant castle. Jonas sent another blast of mental energy towards Malthusius, stunning the cephalopod. Dragon after dragon dove towards the castle, toasting the granite structure with immense heat. In a moment Malthusius recovered enough to start exploding dragons again. As the dragons sped towards the castle Malthusius blew them to pieces, one after another.

Alexander hovered in the air, several hundred feet over Malthusius' immense, roofless house. He could see Malthusius sitting on his throne below and he watched the other dragons attack for several minutes. As he watched, he pondered how best to attack this monster below without being destroyed like his companions, he knew he had one chance. He could see one of Malthusius' eyes was staring straight up at him. Alexander let out a mighty scream and dove towards Malthusius. He let out a white hot flame as he dove. Another mental blast from Jonas hit Malthusius at that moment.

Somewhat stunned, Malthusius lifted several tentacles preparing to ward off the large incoming dragon. Another blast of mental confusion hit the monster. He couldn't get any mental control over the incoming dragon or figure out where the mental attacks were coming from and it was frustrating him. Alexander dodged the waving tentacles. He drove himself into the gaping mouth of Malthusius. He plunged into Malthusius with everything he had, expelling every last bit of flame he had within himself, exploding like a nuclear furnace. A white hot fire erupted. Eleven thousand degrees of searing heat exploded inside of Malthusius and the ancient cephalopod burst into millions of flaming pieces. The song of Malthusius suddenly stopped. The world became silent.

The island of Malthusius, now engulfed in flames, sank below the waves, carrying with it the remains of Malthusius and Alexander. In the mountains of San Bernardino, Jonas removed the helmet from his head, he had a massive headache and his forehead was dripping sweat. After the last mental blast was sent the song had stopped abruptly. As he listened to the silence Jonas could hardly allow himself to hope this meant Malthusius was gone, dead.

-52-
MEANWHILE AND LATER ON

As a quiet settled over the Earth, it took a little bit for everyone to awaken from the hypnotic trance of the songs of Malthusius. Some people never recovered, like Hugo Branson, but that's okay. The world was better for it. Even though there was no longer a background song to rule his life, Hugo remained a kinder and gentler soul.

Der proposed to Paul LePaul at the art opening on June 18th, just a few days after Alexander sacrificed himself to save the world. As expected, the proposal in the middle of the art opening made a big, flamboyant splash. Plans were made to get married that coming October in Joshua Tree at Hicksville Trailer Palace.

Traffic, unfortunately, returned to its normal mess, but wasn't quite as bad as it was before.

Paige and Rufus were back to staying at Remy's place in the hi-desert. Bessie was parked on the side of the house, ready for another adventure. Paige had safely put away about $20,000 earned on the expedition and was still waiting to hear about her disability claim, and to hear from Newsome Whitmore.

Newsome Whitmore disappeared. I'd like to think he'll show up again someday, but for now he's lost in the back country of Alaska.

JP finally visited Remy out in the hi-desert in late July. Every member of the winning hockey team gets to spend a day with the Cup to do whatever they want. JP took the Stanley Cup to Joshua Tree to visit his brother. It seemed like the right thing to do. Remy threw a huge party, like he said he would. Paige was there, of course, and so was Emily, who was beside herself with excitement to drink champagne from the legendary Stanley Cup.

Emily finished her documentary in time for *Dragon Week,* and was now in discussions with JP and the Anaheim Ducks about doing a documentary about a week in the life of an NHL goalie.

Bud Henry and his son Mike spent years working on the Great Pacific Garbage Patch and they were able to reduce its size, but not eliminate it completely. Every year thousands of tons of garbage were added to the pile. As long as that continued the cleanup effort would never be finished. Don Henry finished law school and passed the bar on the first attempt. He became a corporate lawyer for ExxonMobil.

Wolf Thomas and the Joshua Tree chapter of the Church of Malthusius disbanded a few months after the demise of Malthusius. Once the songs stopped most members woke up out of their trance and started to wander off, many of them profoundly changed by their experience. After a month there were only a few members left. All they talked about was the second coming of Malthusius, which they were sure would happen soon.

Cassie Stackwell is still tending bar at the Joshua Tree Saloon. If you stop in, be sure to say hi. She would like that.

As for the dragons, they disappeared soon after Malthusius was destroyed. What happened, as far as we know, was that the remaining thunder of dragons returned to Mount St. Elias, and re-layed their stories of the battle to the others. There was another grand council, and on the advice of Griffin, the Scottish dragon, the plans for war with the humans was put off for another time. The human population can be thankful for that. I'm sure a war between the dragons and the humans would not have gone well for the general population. Soon, "the greatest threat mankind has ever faced" was forgotten about by most everyone, replaced by other news.

I wish I could tell you more about what happened to the dragons, but they simply vanished into remote areas. By the time the military had shown up at Mount St. Elias every single dragon was gone. I imagine they're hiding out in caves, waterholes, lakes, rivers and oceans around the world, avoiding humans. I also imagine they'll be back sometime in the future.

Meanwhile, in the San Bernardino Mountains Jonas Knight put his cabin in order, left a note for his sister, rolled up a joint of JK Special, and stuck it behind his ear. As he stepped out on to the porch he called out for Nathan, who flew over and landed beside him. Jonas and Nathan walked down the path and Jonas closed the gate behind them, then the two disappeared.

JON CHRISTOPHER was born and raised in Southern California. He lives with his love of more than 30 years, Tania, in the hi-desert overlooking Joshua Tree National Park. Jon's either writing, creating music, painting or designing books for Traveling Shoes Press – and always spending time with Suki the dog.

This is Jon's third novel. His debut novel, *Somewhere Out There In The West* was published in the fall of 2017, followed up by his second novel, *Moving At The Speed Of Time*, which came out on April 20th, 2018. He's currently working on his next novel, *Joe's Late Great American Dream*.

OTHER BOOKS FROM TRAVELING SHOES PRESS

Emmy Albertina Bogaerts
Emmy, The Memoir of a Flemish Immigrant

Jon Christopher
Somewhere Out There In The West
Moving At The Speed Of Time
Realistic Hallucinations

Jean-Paul L. Garnier
Echo of Creation

Gabriel Hart
Virgins in Reverse / The Intrusion

Mark Leysen
The Klown

Nora Novak
Los Feliz Confidential, A Memoir

TRAVELINGSHOESPRESS.COM

www.ingramcontent.com/pod-product-compliance
Lightning Source LLC
Chambersburg PA
CBHW020435180626
46812CB00003B/1252